A Meeting in the Ladies' Room

ANITA DOREEN DIGGS

DAFINA BOOKS
Kensington Publishing Corp.
http://www.kensingtonbooks.com

A Meeting
in the
Ladies' Room

ACKNOWLEDGMENTS

I'd like to thank Professor Michael Hyde at the State University of New York Fashion Institute of Technology (F.I.T.) for his wisdom, guidance, and enthusiasm for this story.

"The price one pays for pursuing any profession, or calling, is an intimate knowledge of its ugly side."

James Baldwin
Nobody Knows My Name, 1961

CONTENTS

Contents

I

VICTOR IN THE SKY . . .
WITH DIAMONDS

Blackmail is a despicable act, and I only stooped that low because my alternative was to spend twenty-five years in prison for a murder that I didn't commit. My name is Jacqueline Blue, and I'm really a decent woman. I obey the laws of New York State even when they don't make sense. I support my mother, who, because she didn't finish high school and has no skills, can't find a job. I contribute to the NAACP even though they hold more banquets than protests during these last years of the twentieth century. I also respect the privacy of my fellow human beings. So, if someone had told me a year ago that I would dig into the background of a *New York Comet* reporter and uncover secrets to force her cooperation in my affairs, I would have laughed uncontrollably.

My biggest problems at the beginning of this year were my unrequited love for a traveling salesman named Victor Bell and editing an offensive biography written by Craig Murray, an untalented scribe who was married to my boss. It was a lonely existence, but I figured that once Craig's book was completed and Victor had come to his senses, my life would become paradise. God had other plans.

It was the middle of January and so cold outside that my ears, fingers, and toes grew numb during the ten minutes it took to walk from the office building where I worked in Times Square to B. Smith's restaurant for the weekly Black Pack get-together.

We called ourselves the Black Pack because the eight of us were the only African-American professionals working in the rarefied world of Manhattan book publishing. Each of us worked for a different company. We had nothing in common except a shared cultural heritage and a need to vent about the frustration, alienation, and invalidation that we experienced from some members of the Dominant Culture. At the end of each dangerously soul-sapping, energy-draining week, it was nice to take off our Corporate Negro masks and relax.

I can still see myself, pulling off a heavy red wool cape and matching gloves as I followed the hostess to a round table where five members of the group were already seated. My hair was freshly braided, curled, and hanging loose around my shoulders. I was wearing a square-necked, long-sleeved red dress, belted at the waist, which had cost way too much money but looked so good on my buxom, five-foot, five-inch frame that it was guaranteed to show off my coffee-colored skin and make Victor sweat.

Victor wasn't there and my heart sank, even as the others greeted me cheerfully. Paul Dodson caught my eye and knew my instant misery. Paul was the only one in the group that knew about my crush on our colleague.

Alyssa was missing also. Our workloads made it impossible for all eight of us to show up every single Friday night. I sat down, hoping that Victor would stop by later.

Rachel was there, dressed to the nines and batting her eyelashes at each male who passed by the table. Everyone in the group knew that the only reason Rachel Edwards never missed a gathering was that she was desperate to find a rich husband and B. Smith's attracted its share of professional Black men. Rachel was one of the few black publicists in the business, but she didn't care about us, Black book buyers, or anyone except herself. She longed for a luxurious house, set on a few acres of land in Westchester County, where she could hobnob with the wives of other rich men and spend the rest of her time serving on committees. She was a pathetic gold digger who had recently dyed her hair blond to match.

Sitting across the table from Rachel, I tried not to notice her flashing smiles in the direction of several brothers in business suits who were having drinks at the bar to the left of our table. A pretty and petite woman just past her thirtieth birthday, Rachel was wearing a black knit dress that clung to her curves. I know this because she got up several times during the evening to go to the bathroom so that the men could watch her glide.

"Why Jackie, don't you look sensational in that red dress," she said with a smile.

"It is definitely working," Joe Long agreed.

"I'll bet it's a Nicole Miller," said Elaine "I went to Harvard" Garner.

Elaine was one of the most irritating people I had ever met. She had a habit of bringing up her Ivy League education at every possible opportunity. It was my boss, Annabelle Murray, who had nicknamed her Elaine "I went to Harvard" Garner, and I shared that information with Paul, who laughed himself silly. People in the industry made a game of getting off the phone before she could mention Harvard and avoided as much social interaction with her as possible. The Black Pack couldn't do that because she was . . . well . . . Black.

"Probably a Nicole Miller knockoff," observed Dallas Mowrey as she poked at a slice of lime in her drink.

For a split second I felt like scratching Dallas's eyes out, but suppose Victor was simply running late? It just wouldn't do for him to find me in an ugly catfight with that fat, pockmark-faced, cross-eyed, just-bought-a-brownstone-but-don't-have-enough-money to-put-a-decent-roof-on-it little bitch.

He was a very quiet, sophisticated, intelligent gentleman who would never date me after witnessing a scene like that.

I glanced over my shoulder just to make sure Victor wasn't approaching the table before I said, "Go to hell, Dallas."

A waiter took my drink order as Rachel giggled nervously and Paul tapped the side of his water glass with a knife. "Ladies, ladies, we've come together for good food, strong drink, and Black unity. I'm not feeling any sisterly love here."

Paul was trying hard not to chuckle—the sight of his cheeks all puffed up with the effort made us laugh.

Joe Long peered at me over the top of his glasses. "Congratulations on signing Jamal Hunt." Joe was a slim, bespectacled, nervous-looking editor who specialized in books on slavery, segregation, and the civil rights movement because the editorial board at the company he worked for wouldn't let him buy anything else. He was smart, reclusive, and good-looking in a tweedy, college professor kind of way.

"We didn't bid in that auction," Joe continued, "but I knew that the major houses were going to battle hard to win his next two books."

Acquiring Jamal Hunt's next two books was a definite feather in my cap. He was the crown prince of hip-hop-flavored fiction.

"Thanks, Joe," I replied. "That damned auction dragged on for two days."

"Who was the agent?" asked Rachel.

"Penelope Aaron."

We all shared a collective groan. Penelope was the nastiest, most abrasive literary agent in the business. All the editors, black and white, hated her guts but she was particularly galling to members of the Black Pack. She was a white woman who had an all-Black stable of writers only because authors of her own race absolutely refused to deal with her. They thought she was stupid, incompetent, and low class.

I didn't think Penelope was stupid. Duplicitous and conniving, yes. But not stupid.

What pissed me off was the sassy, singsong, pseudo-southern voice and bits of Black vernacular she threw into her conversations in an effort to bond with me. It was insulting; I wasn't having it and once told her so in no uncertain terms. Since her writers found her misguided attempts at Blackness amusing and the other Black editors never told her how they really felt, she could not understand my position.

Dallas said, "Girl, you have got your hands full! Jamal Hunt thinks he is God's gift to the literary community and, as quiet as it's kept, I had to rewrite most of that shit when I was his editor."

I wanted to know more about those rewrites, but how would it look if I talked against my own client? Defending Jamal was the only professional thing to do. I took a long swig of my Bacardi 'n' Coke. "Actually, I've spoken to him once and he seems kind of sweet, and besides, his last book sold eighty thousand copies in hardcover."

Dallas ran a chubby, bejeweled hand through her hair. "Jamal is a pain in the ass."

The waiter reappeared for our food orders. B. Smith's

specializes in what Paul calls "nouveau soul food." I ordered the macaroni and cheese with Thai chicken wings.

"I'm going to wash my hands," Rachel said. Dallas and Elaine had to get up because Rachel was squished between them.

Dallas waited until Rachel was out of earshot. "Why the hell doesn't she just go over there, ask one of those guys out, and be done with it? This is ridiculous."

"She really needs to stop that shit," Elaine grumbled. "When she gets back, I'm going to tell her to sit somewhere else. Jackie, why don't you trade places with Rachel?"

"And have me getting up and down like a jack-in-the-box?" asked Paul. "No way."

I ignored their childish little squabble.

The restaurant was large and airy with about two dozen tables carefully arranged so that diners could speak without being overheard. The place was owned by a former fashion model named Barbara Smith who was the first Black woman to appear on the cover of *Mademoiselle* magazine. That cover and many others had been blown up and now graced the walls of her restaurant. I had also seen her in TV commercials for Revlon, Clairol, and Noxzema and as a guest on *The Today Show* and *Good Morning America*. She was one of the few Black women who wrote entertainment and lifestyle books for a major publishing house. As I gazed at the magazine covers featuring this talented and gorgeous creature, a little sigh escaped me.

"You will never look like that," Paul said, teasing me.

"And you'll never look like Denzel Washington either," I retorted.

We both laughed.

"Actually, I think Jackie is a very handsome woman," Dallas said.

It was an insult disguised as a compliment. I flashed a

smile in her direction. "Thank you, Dallas. I admire the way you find such fashionable clothes on the plus-size rack."

"Cease fire!" commanded Paul.

Elaine casually asked Paul if Victor had called to say he wasn't coming.

"Nah, I didn't hear from him. I guess he is out on the road."

"I think our Victor has made himself a love connection," Dallas said, laughing.

My heart sank. "What makes you say that?"

"I saw him coming out of Victoria's Secret over on Madison Avenue last week. He was alone and carrying two shopping bags of stuff. We talked for a minute but he wouldn't tell me who the lucky girl is."

Dallas thrived on gossip and it didn't take much to get her started on the personal dramas of other people. Paying attention to her stories provided more entertainment than a Hollywood melodrama.

Victor was funny, single, intelligent, well read, handsome, and polished. I wasn't interested in hearing any sordid tales about my dream man, but Joe stopped her before I could.

Joe slammed his glass down on the table. "I swear, you are such a vicious gossip! I'm surprised you didn't just assume that Victor is a cross-dresser and start spreading that dirt around!"

I had never seen Joe get angry before and his reaction was so extreme that no one knew what to say. It was clear from the expression of murderous rage on his face that Dallas had unwittingly stumbled into dangerous territory, but that didn't make sense unless Joe had a crush on the same "lucky girl."

I downed my rum and Coke in one gulp—and half of Paul's Scotch. The combination made me wince.

In due course the whole world would know Victor's

secret and it would rock us to our very foundations, but that night I was still determined to become his woman and this information caused a new heaviness to curl up around my heart.

"What on earth is the matter with you?" Elaine asked finally.

"Nothing," Joe replied shortly. "Excuse me." He headed toward the men's room.

"I'm confused," said Rachel. "What just happened here?"

There was a lot of murmuring around the table about Joe's astonishing behavior, but I wasn't listening to any of it. Dallas was indeed a gossip, but once in a while her information was accurate and this made Victor's consistent rejection of my overtures during the past year even harder to swallow. I ordered myself two drinks from a passing waiter.

Paul whispered in my ear, "What's the matter, Jackie?"

"I wonder who Victor was buying underwear for and whether it's just a fling or if the woman really means something to him," I whispered back.

Paul made a tsk-tsk sound and then said, "It's time you and I had a talk."

Whatever he wanted to say to me would have to wait. Elaine was starting the "let's bitch about white folks" hour.

"Did you hear what happened to Alyssa Kraft?"

Alyssa was one of us. A tall, slender, copper-skinned sister from St. Louis, she was a genius at fixing even the purplest of prose. She was also kind, charitable, and sweet.

Joe slid back into his seat. "What about Alyssa?"

Elaine took a sip of her Bailey's and said, "Alyssa went to some thousand-dollar-a-plate fund-raiser in D.C. a few months ago and she was seated next to Davina Coolidge."

Paul whistled. Davina Coolidge was the highest-ranking African-American in President Clinton's administration.

"They did the polite chitchat thing and it turned to girl talk. At the end of the evening, they exchanged phone numbers. Every time Davina came to New York, she called Alyssa for dinner or drinks. Whenever Alyssa was in D.C. visiting her folks, she called Davina."

"Wow!" said Dallas.

"At some point, Alyssa suggested that Davina's rags-to-riches story would make a terrific inspirational memoir. At first Davina said no, but she eventually changed her mind. So, Alyssa helped her write a short proposal and presented it at her editorial meeting this week. Well, Marlena Rashker, the executive editor, told Alyssa that she had done a fantastic job, but since the project had ties to the White House, she would have to share it with Marlena."

"What a load of crap," I said.

"I know Marlena Rashker," said Paul. "She is going to take all the credit, have her name in all the press coverage, and push Alyssa so far back in the process, even Davina won't remember her existence."

"Ah," Elaine replied, pointing her swizzle stick in Paul's direction. "Our Alyssa must have known something like that would happen and told Davina to expect it. Well, to Davina's credit, she had instructed Alyssa to announce at the meeting that her editor had to be an African-American or she would find another publishing house."

We were all grinning and cheering by now and even Rachel stopped batting her eyes at the men who were drinking at the bar. Our whooping and hollering provoked quite a few reproving stares from our fellow diners, but we didn't care.

Joe murmured, "That took a lot of guts. I wouldn't have had the nerve to say it."

Elaine held up her hand for silence. "I'm not through.

When Alyssa made that statement, Rashker went wild. She stood up and screamed at Alyssa in front of everyone."

I was surprised. "What exactly did she say?"

"She yelled, 'Who the hell do you think you are?'"

There was a gasp from Dallas. "Oh my God, poor Alyssa."

"No shit," agreed Paul.

"Alyssa," continued Elaine, "just sat there like a pillar of concrete. My contact over there told me that she seemed literally incapable of movement or speech. The woman told Alyssa point-blank that she better not ever pull a stunt like that again . . . that there was no such thing as black editing or white editing . . . that Alyssa better hope the book earned out its advance or she was going to be pounding the sidewalk looking for some more black editing to do."

"Get the fuck outta here!" Paul exclaimed in disbelief. "Even if that's what she was thinking, I can't believe Marlena Rashker would be stupid enough to say it in front of a room full of witnesses."

There was a general murmur of agreement.

"This is really bad," said Joe, "but there is a silver lining to this cloud."

We all wanted to know what on earth it was.

Joe steepled his fingers and what he said next made perfect sense. "Alyssa Kraft is the only member of the Black Pack who is guaranteed a job for the next hundred years. She won't be downsized, outsized, or anything else. This stupid woman, whoever she is, just opened the company up to a gigantic racial discrimination lawsuit and the powers that be over there are going to make sure that our Alyssa is kept very happy."

"Apparently Alyssa didn't share your optimism," Elaine finished triumphantly. "She quit her job the next morning."

"Does anyone have her home phone number?" I asked. "This is terrible. We've all got to do something."

"Like what?" asked Elaine. "She is a grown woman who decided that she would prefer to work elsewhere. She wasn't fired. I say we all stay out of it."

"I agree," Joe said.

"Me, too," Dallas chimed in. "The last thing I need is a bunch of angry white people breathing down my neck."

Paul said nothing, and by the look on his face I knew that he agreed with Dallas.

Elaine cleared her throat. "There is one other thing."

A leopard just cannot change its spots. I knew what was coming.

"There is no way Davina Coolidge is going to sign with them after what happened, so I wouldn't be stabbing Alyssa in the back if I took a trip to D.C. and met with her, would I?"

"What time does your flight leave, Elaine?" I asked softly.

"I'm taking the shuttle first thing Monday morning." Elaine looked around at our angry faces and her expression became defiant. "Look, this is a business. That is what I learned at Harvard."

Even though it was still early, none of us was in the mood to party any longer. Paul tapped a fork on his glass and shouted, "Okay, folks. On that note, I must take my leave. What is my share of the bill?"

I stood up, too. "Yes, it has been interesting. Good night."

The atmosphere was tense and I knew that the rest of the group would break up before I was halfway home.

We all air-kissed and waved good-bye. I kept a fake smile on my face until Paul and I were out on the sidewalk, and then my emotions got the better of me. Tears slid down my face. "Jesus, what a night! Victor might be taken and now Alyssa is unemployed."

Paul gave me a handkerchief. "Jackie, I hope you don't get mad at me for what I'm about to say, but I'm your best friend and it's time I came out with it."

Paul and I had bonded instantly at a book party a few years before and quickly become almost inseparable. We shared our secrets, dreams, and problems. He had my back and I most definitely had his.

"Just say what you have to say," I sniffled.

"Okay." He took a deep breath and held my chin up so we were staring into each other's eyes. "I don't know how or why it happened, but you are obsessed with Victor Bell and you need professional help."

"I'm not mad at you, Paul."

He looked relieved. "Good. Now let me help you get a taxi."

We walked to the corner of Eighth Avenue and stood there shivering in the frigid air until an empty cab appeared. Paul promised to find Alyssa's number, kissed me good-bye, and I got in. My thoughts immediately returned to my dream man. Why wasn't Victor attracted to me? Did he prefer tall women? Light skinned sisters? What could I do that I hadn't already done to let him know that I wanted him? The questions went round and round in my head, the liquor sent me into a crying jag, and I wept all the way home to Harlem. I should have saved my tears for something more worthwhile—like the two nights I would spend in police custody.

2

ROSA WITH THE CROOKED NOSE

Paul's older brother, Richard, had recently opened a soul food restaurant around the corner from my apartment. Paul spent a lot of time helping out there on the weekends when he wasn't sprawled out on my sofa, watching TV and reading manuscripts. He called me the next morning.

"Hello," I croaked.

"Jackie, your voice sounds like fingernails rasping on sandpaper. Do you have a hangover?"

"Aargh."

"I'll come up after the breakfast rush and take care of you, okay?"

"I need water. What time is it?"

"Ten o'clock."

"Okay."

I live in a one-bedroom apartment on 111th Street in Harlem. When you enter my place, you are in the living room. There is a tweed sofa set against the long wall with a wood coffee table in front of it and matching tables on each side that hold my two kitschy Coca-Cola lamps. I have a computer hutch on another wall where my laptop sits and a bookcase in a corner that holds about fifty books.

There is a short hallway on the right. The walk-in kitchen and my bathroom are on the left.

Straight ahead is my bedroom, which holds a platform bed with built-in night tables and two pull-out drawers underneath. I have a framed picture of my boss, Annabelle Murray, and me with our arms around Denzel Washington on one night table. The photo was taken at the National Book Awards three years ago. He was kind and gracious about posing with us, although he did turn down Annabelle's offer of three million dollars in exchange for a totally candid autobiography.

A television with a built-in VCR sits on a stand with wheels slightly to the left of my bed.

There is a picture of Mama on one living room wall. Otherwise, the walls in my apartment are bare.

I hung up and stumbled into the bathroom, so thirsty that I cupped my hands and drank from the faucet in the sink before washing my face. My face in the mirror almost made me gag. The eyes were swollen from crying and black eyeliner had run down onto my cheeks. The effect was that of a tragic clown.

After swallowing two aspirins and enduring a cold shower, I felt human enough to check my messages. Mama had called. She wanted to know when I was coming to see her. I dialed her back.

"Hi, Mama, how are you?"

"Okay. Are you coming downtown today?"

"I can't, Mama. I have to work."

"At your boss's apartment again?"

"Yeah. I have to be there at two o'clock."

"Why can't you come see me when you leave there?"

"Because Craig Murray's bad writing gets on my last

nerve and after three hours of him, I won't be good company for anyone."

"Oh."

The "Oh" was so sad.

"I'll tell you what. Why don't I come over tomorrow and spend the night at your house?"

She perked up immediately. "All right. I'll make stewed chicken, dumplings, and collard greens. We'll have a real old-fashioned Sunday dinner."

"It sounds wonderful, Mama."

"How is Paul?"

"Fine, Mama. I saw him last night."

"Tell him I said hello."

"Okay."

"Is your boss paying you extra money for helping her husband?"

Mama had asked me this before. "No, but she really appreciates it and she has said that something real sweet lies ahead for me. I'm hoping it's a promotion to executive editor."

"Real sweet, huh? What if she just gives you a box of chocolates?" Mama laughed heartily at her own joke.

"I'll wring her scrawny neck," I answered with a chuckle that made my head hurt even more. "Do you need me to bring you anything tomorrow?"

"Some oranges and grapes would be nice."

"Okay. I love you, Mama."

"I love you too, honey."

I had just lotioned myself up and slipped into jeans, sneakers, and a navy blue turtleneck sweater when Paul arrived. He was carrying two bags of food, which I snatched from his hands before he had locked my front door behind him.

What is there to say about Paul? He is average-looking—tall, light-skinned, and stocky with close-cropped, wavy hair. Aside from his brother Richard, he had no family. His mother died when he was ten and the boys had never known their father. Paul and his brother had grown up in the foster care system.

He followed me into the kitchen and watched as I tore into the cartons.

"I didn't know what you were in the mood for, so there are four different meals. Fried chicken and waffles. Grits, bacon, and biscuits. Fried catfish and grits. Bacon, eggs, and toast."

"This is wonderful, Paul, but . . ."

"But the smell is making you feel queasy all of a sudden and you're wishing for some tea and dry toast instead, am I right?"

I gave him a grateful smile. "What would I do without you?"

"You'll never have to find out." He opened the refrigerator door and packed the food neatly onto the shelves. "You also won't have to cook for a week. Go lie down."

I threw myself across the bed, wishing that there was some way I could get out of going to see Annabelle and Craig on my day off. Sleep had overtaken me again when Paul woke me up. The tea and toast were on my nightstand.

His light brown eyes watched me intently as I bit a piece of the toast. "Jackie, the only reason you got so drunk is because you were disappointed that Victor didn't show up. You really need to think about what I said last night."

My face creased into a frown.

"You've been torturing yourself over this guy for the past year."

"I'm going to end this torture by calling Victor and inviting him over."

Paul's eyebrows went up. "For what?"

"Toe-curling sex, followed by lots of cuddling. What else?"

"Very funny." He gave me an odd look and then said, "Guess who asked me out?"

"The waitress with the crooked nose who used to work for Richard?"

"Her name is Rosa and her nose is not crooked."

The girl's nose was definitely bent but I wasn't going to argue the point. Now that I'd consumed the tea and toast it was time for Paul to leave so I could get some more sleep before heading downtown to the Murrays'.

Once I'd been in the restaurant and watched as Rosa hung on Paul's every word. Her eyes followed him around the restaurant with such naked admiration that he had started showing off—barking orders to the lone waitress so loudly that Helen Keller could have heard him and moving tables like a busboy to show off his muscles.

Unfortunately, Rosa had to quit when she lost the woman who babysat her two children, but Paul told me that she had pressed her number into his hand before leaving.

"It's really nice to meet a woman who is working so hard to better herself. She wants to go to college and study the restaurant business."

"Miss Rosa wants to study the Paul Dodson business so he can marry her and she won't need college," I corrected him. "I watched her. She was looking at you with gold in her eyes."

"Baloney. I'm fine as hell and she wants me," Paul said, pointing at his chest.

"Really? Boy, has she run a number on your head. Soon, you'll be telling me there isn't anything you won't do for dear, dear Rosa."

Paul stood and picked up my dirty dishes. "That won't happen but there is nothing I won't do for my dear, dear Jackie." He paused on the way to the kitchen. "So, should I go out with her?"

"Sure, have fun."

Paul had had a crush on me for the past three years and I had always pretended not to know it so I didn't have to hurt his feelings. He wasn't my type, and if the issue was ever pulled from beneath the surface of our friendship, I would have to tell him the truth. He would flee in pain and humiliation. I loved having him in my life too much to let that happen. We were on dangerous ground.

He looked disappointed. "Fine. Do you need anything else?"

"No, go on back to the restaurant and let me get some more sleep. I'm due at my boss's house in two hours."

At the door, Paul fished around in his pocket and came up with a slip of paper. "Here is Alyssa's number."

He left without another word.

I never did go back to sleep. After Paul left, I rehearsed three different speeches to recite when Victor answered his phone. Then I got scared. If he rejected me voice to voice, I wouldn't be able to handle it. It seemed better to proposition him via computer.

Before I could lose my nerve, I composed an e-mail that said:

Hi, Handsome,
   Sorry you missed the Black Pack meeting last night. I was looking forward to seeing you. Suppose we both skip next Friday's gathering and get together alone at my place. I'll wear something sheer and pour Dom Perignon into real crystal glasses while we . . . er . . . talk.

And then I clicked the SEND button.

3

ALL ABOUT MOMS

Hell's Kitchen is a nickname for the area in Manhattan that stretches north from 34th Street to 59th Street and west from Eighth Avenue to the Hudson River. This is where I was born and raised. The funny thing is that I never heard the term "Hell's Kitchen" until I was a grown woman sitting in a job interview. The interviewer noted my address and said, "Hmmm, a Hell's Kitchen girl."

We called our neighborhood "Clinton."

It really doesn't matter what your community is called if you're poor. The people of Clinton were poor whites, poor Puerto Ricans, and a smattering of poor Blacks, which included me and Mama.

To be poor in an area where there is need and want spreading around you for miles in each direction is one thing, but to grow up poor in Clinton was another because we could see and smell the riches wafting over from Broadway, Sixth Avenue, Fifth Avenue, and Park Avenue. Some of our neighbors would sit on the stoop and talk about moving east when their ship came in, but Mama didn't. She never believed that a ship would come in for her and refused to waste time thinking about it.

Mama didn't like her lot in life but she accepted it calmly. In fact, she still lived in the same apartment that I'd grown up in. Mama refused to come stay with me, preferring to stick to familiar ground where she was the woman in charge. It made my chest tighten up every time I entered the shabby building.

As for me, I decided early on that no ship was going to pull up in front of the Radio City Station post office across the street from our tenement, so I would have to swim out to sea and jump on the first vessel that came into view. It took a series of dead-end secretarial jobs following college for me to land in the right industry. But once I was bitten by the publishing bug, I worked very hard, changed companies twice for career advancement, and finally got the position I wanted.

How I went from book editor to accused murderer is the stuff TV miniseries are made of. I've had a lot of time over the past few months to ponder this journey and the media has used up a lot of ink trying to dissect it.

I was born Jacqueline Naomi Blue, only surviving child (the first one, a boy, was stillborn) of Quincy and Mozelle Blue, in St. Clare's Hospital right down the street from the tenement. A year after my birth, Daddy ran off with Mama's best friend and we never heard from him again.

Mama raised me to keep my legs closed, my mouth shut, and to never betray a friend. She had come to New York from Memphis, Tennessee, and even though her family begged her to come home after Daddy left, she just couldn't. Apparently they had told her he was a no-good creep and she'd be sorry for running off with him. Since her parents had died long ago, Mama figured that nothing was left for her back in Memphis but three sisters who were waiting with mouths chock-full of I-told-you-sos.

She was only twenty years old when I was born but sorrow, bitterness, and shock have a way of aging a woman so that by the time Mama was thirty, she looked forty. She and I lived a pretty solitary life. She worked as a cashier for Met Supermarket from the time Daddy left until they tore the store down three years ago. I've been supporting her since then and I don't mind at all.

Mama has a picture of herself taken in Memphis about two years before Daddy came through town and swept her off her feet. Her eyes are glowing with hope, her hair swept up in an elaborate roll, the lips parted, showing perfect teeth.

She is still beautiful but the hope for her own life has been replaced by the pride she feels in my accomplishment.

Mama never told me that we were poor. It took a brief childhood friendship to teach me that.

There was one white girl in my fifth-grade class who was not poor. Her name was Mandy and she, too, lived in a single-parent household. Mandy's mother acted in TV commercials and received alimony and child support from Mandy's father, whose occupation I never knew. When Mandy invited me over to her house, which was on 55th Street between Eighth and Ninth Avenue, I had to beg Mama to let me go. I understand now that Mama was trying to protect me from the sting of racism. After my visit, I naturally invited Mandy back to play at our house. Her mother wouldn't hear of it and our friendship ended soon after.

Their place was huge. Until then, I had never seen an apartment with more than one bathroom. The ceilings were so high that I couldn't figure out how Mandy's mother changed the light-bulb. There was thick carpeting on the floors instead of cracked linoleum, pictures in heavy frames on the walls, and floor-to-ceiling book-cases, which held important looking volumes. But it was the air in that living space that made the greatest impression on me. Or rather, what was not in the air. There were no clouds of disappointment, anxiety, desperation, or bitterness in that air and I breathed deeply, trying to fill my lungs with it.

There are particular times in life that you can recall with crystal clarity, and I never forgot that moment in time when I stood in Mandy's living room with my little chest heaving up and down, trying to gather up enough of that air so I could let some of it out into our place later on.

I tried to explain Mandy's air to Mama, but she didn't understand.

On the way over to Craig and Annabelle Murray's house that Saturday morning, I knew that the air would greet me as soon as I entered their building. I now knew the smell for what it was—the odor of security.

The Murrays lived on Manhattan's Upper West Side in an enormous, castle-like apartment building called The Dakota. It was built in 1884, boasted a fountain in its courtyard, and folks like Lauren Bacall and Yoko Ono are just two examples of its illustrious tenants.

One of several passenger elevators took me up to their eighth-floor penthouse. The door opened and I was in the vestibule of their apartment. Annabelle answered the bell. She was a tall, leggy blonde in her early forties who looked much younger and was proud that people frequently stopped her on the street asking for an autograph. Annabelle had once won a celebrity look-alike contest for her astonishing resemblance to the actress Daryl Hannah. She was wearing a hunter-green turtleneck sweater, matching slacks, and Prada loafers.

As she embraced me, she said, "Hey, Jackie, come on in! Craig has a big surprise for you!"

Annabelle was one of the best publishers in the business and during the five years I'd worked at Welburn Books, I'd had nothing but respect for her editorial judgment. After she coerced me into helping her husband with his biography of the great Black comedienne, Jackie "Moms" Mabley, I discovered that the old saying, "love is blind," was totally true. Craig Murray had absolutely no writing talent and Annabelle was too in love with him to see it. The best surprise he could have for me was an announcement that he'd thrown his manuscript in the garbage. But of course I couldn't say that and expect to remain employed, so I summoned up a bright smile and replied, "This is so exciting. I can't wait to read the new pages!"

She marched briskly ahead of me through the foyer, a gigantic, unfurnished area with a polished wood floor and dozens of framed pictures of their three-year-old daughter, Dora, on the sea-green walls.

After taking my coat, Annabelle waved me on. "Craig is waiting for you in the library. I'll see you in an hour or two. Dora and I are going to Bloomingdale's."

Craig is basically a nice guy but I couldn't tolerate his literary pretensions on a full bladder, so a quick stop in the bathroom was in order. I knew from my first tour of Annabelle's ten-room apartment that this bathroom, which was all pink—including tile, marble floor, octagon-shaped tub, and double-basin sink—was the guest bathroom and as I sat on the baby-pink toilet, I marveled at the fact that the space was bigger than my bedroom.

The library was exactly that. Floor-to-ceiling bookshelves made up the four walls and there was a long conference-room sized table in the middle of the room with six chairs on each side of it. The floor had a red carpet which was the only hint of color in the very functional research-and-reading space. Craig was already seated, pencil behind his ear, shuffling papers around. He stood up and welcomed me with a smile that showed the huge gap between his two front teeth. He was a tall, gangly man with dirty yellow hair that hung to his shoulders, hippie style, who had been wearing jeans and a white tee shirt every time we met. That day was no exception.

"Craig, good to see you!" I waved him back down, sat across the table from him, and pulled my Filofax and a pen out of my tote bag to take notes. "I hear you have a surprise for me."

He slapped the table and laughed. "Annabelle just can't keep a secret. Yes, Jackie, it's true. I've finished the last hundred pages of *All About Moms*. My wife has read them and pronounced me brilliant. Of course, she is prejudiced in my favor."

He chuckled. I chuckled.

"So, I'm going to leave you alone to peruse this lengthy piece of prose while I rustle us up some grub, okay?" Craig slid the stack of paper across the table, gave me the thumbs-up sign, and left me alone in the library, closing the door behind him. It took me an hour to get through his latest twaddle and by that time, my annoyance had changed to heated resentment.

From the beginning, Craig's narrative had shown that he did not understand the humor of Jackie Mabley, life on the chitlin' circuit where she was forced to earn her living during the early years of her career, or why present-day African-American comics like Chris Rock and Eddie Murphy revered her.

Now, at the end of his book, Craig was blaming one of the funniest women in the world for "not reaching the white audience which could have made her a superstar because, instead of running after this golden purse, Moms preferred to pursue young black men, as evidenced by one of her most famous jokes: *The only thing an old man can do for me is show me which way a young one went.*

I felt like flipping one of the pages over and using it to write my resignation from Welburn Books. Instead, I opened my Filofax, blocked out a few hours of time to edit the pages, sent up a silent prayer for sister Mabley, and, like a good Corporate Negro, kept my eyes on the executive editor prize.

4

A THIN PINK LINE

Craig and I munched on homemade pizza and drank cold Welch's grape juice in the Murrays' cavernous dining room. Although we made small talk about an assortment of innocent topics—the history of The Dakota apartment building, Dora's ballet lessons, carpeted versus wood floors, the Disneyfication of Times Square, jogging, new restaurants, yo-yo dieting, the latest releases from Welburn Books, and the like—we were surreptitiously killing time until Annabelle returned to lead the book discussion.

Craig apparently knew quite a bit about my work. He made it clear that Annabelle respected the passionate way I shepherded the books in my care through the maze of individual fiefdoms that were the marketing, art, and subsidiary rights departments. He tactfully avoided the fact that I focused exclusively on books by African-American authors, but it wouldn't have bothered me if he had mentioned it. It was my choice—one that I'd made eight years before while working as an editorial assistant at Brigsbay Press.

He told me what I already knew from the office

grapevine—that he had come to New York from a small town in Wisconsin thirteen years ago with dreams of becoming a famous painter. He had met Annabelle Welburn when she attended a reception in his honor at a small art gallery downtown in Soho. They married six months later and he continued the struggling artist bit for five more years before giving it up to write biographies of unsung Americans. What he did not tell me—but what I already knew—was that he wrote two books, one on Sylvia Plath and the other about Allan Ginsberg, which had been rejected by every publishing house in the country—before picking on poor Moms Mabley.

Craig had now entered the fantastic world inhabited by white folks like Penelope Aaron. Folks who had been pegged as talentless in their own community but knew that their color made them top shelf in the Black arena. There was no doubt in my mind that as a white man writing about an unexplored Black subject, Craig would get a lucrative book deal even though he didn't understand the subtleties, nuances, or cultural markers of what he was writing about. I stuffed bitterness into my mouth with every single bite of pizza.

Craig and I were still there when Annabelle materialized. I was struck again by her feminine mannerisms and youthful, almost ethereal, beauty. Dora trailed behind her and stood motionless as Annabelle kissed her husband, waved at me, and then flopped into a chair.

Dora was a pretty child who didn't resemble either of her parents. She had an olive complexion, thick, black, curly hair which fell to her shoulders, and dark brown eyes. I remembered Annabelle's difficult pregnancy so I knew that Dora wasn't adopted but she definitely resembled a little Gypsy.

Craig, wearing a look of concern, waved his daughter closer to the table. "What's the matter, Pixie?"

Dora didn't move. "Mommy says I have to go to the doctor's again. I don't want any more needles."

Craig looked anxiously at Annabelle. "What doctor has Pixie been going to? What is she talking about?"

Annabelle gave her child a shut-the-fuck-up-or-die look and said, "We'll talk about all this later, Dora. It is impolite to make a guest feel uncomfortable in your home. Now say hello to Jackie."

The last thing I needed was to be in the middle of some family drama. Thankfully, Dora heeded her mother's words by giving me an obedient little wave, which I returned.

"Are you hungry, Dora? There is plenty of pizza left," Craig said, smiling.

Dora shook her head and ran from the room.

Annabelle turned her attention to me. "What did you think of the ending?"

I chose my words carefully. "It needs some work, but have you ever seen a manuscript that didn't?" I chuckled and took a sip of grape juice.

Craig looked unhappy. "How much work?"

"A few tucks here and there."

Annabelle nodded. "Okay, tell Craig where to tuck."

I took a deep breath. "Craig, you might want to re-think one thread of the narrative that some readers might find offensive. In other words, you seem to feel that Moms Mabley should have changed her entire act into one that would appeal to white audiences."

No one said anything, so I took a huge gulp of grape juice and plunged on. "You also might want to take another look at the idea that Moms Mabley used up a lot of energy pursuing young Black men, which adversely impacted her career."

"Do you find that offensive as well?" Craig asked mildly.

Moms was pleading with me from heaven to help

keep this ridiculous thesis from ever seeing the light of day. "It just isn't true," I said flatly.

Annabelle's mouth had stretched into a Thin Pink Line. A line that Blacks from the Big House to the Boardroom knew all too well. The line meant that I had only seconds to get back in My Place or there was going to be trouble.

I understood the Thin Pink Line but Annabelle should not have used it in this instance. She had four other senior editors on staff and the only reason I had been chosen over them was because Moms Mabley and I were both African-American. It made perfect sense and there was absolutely nothing wrong with it, but to pick me for my Black sensibility and then give me the Thin Pink Line when I delivered it was totally absurd.

"There is nothing in Craig's research to support such an assertion," I said calmly. "What happened was that Craig gathered some material that he interpreted in the wrong way because he didn't understand certain cultural nuances, but I can fix it for him."

Craig said, "Well, if Jackie Mabley did not become a superstar because of her own uncontrolled lust for young men and a refusal to create material that whites could relate to, what do you say is the cause of her failure?"

"Well, first of all, I don't consider Moms Mabley a failure, but racism certainly played a huge part in her life."

Annabelle shook her head so hard that for a moment the silky, blond strands formed a swirling halo around her head. "We don't want to fall back on that old saw. I also feel that if Craig writes that Miss Mabley's problems were due to racism, that will diminish her as a woman."

Say what?

My heart was pounding and I focused on the way

Mama relied on me to pay for her rent, utilities, food, medicine, and social activities, the thousands of dollars I owed on my five charge accounts, and the fact that there was no other place for me to work at my trade where I wouldn't encounter this same type of bullshit. I focused on these things and then pasted on my Corporate Negro smile. The Thin Pink Line disappeared, and Craig stopped frowning.

"Perhaps you're right, Annabelle. I didn't think about it that way."

Craig grinned widely. "This calls for a celebration. Why don't I uncork a bottle of chilled champagne?"

I stood up and stretched. "That sounds wonderful, but I promised my mother a visit today. I haven't seen her in almost two weeks." The lies flowed smoothly from my lips.

"We can drink rivers of champagne after you sign your first publishing contract, my dear," Annabelle said. "Right now, I have to make some phone calls."

Craig shrugged, although he was visibly disappointed. "Okay, I'll go in and see what's eating Dora."

"No!" Annabelle shouted. "Dora is probably sleeping by now. Besides, I need you to run out and get some eggs. We're having omelets tonight."

It occurred to me that Annabelle was keeping some secret concerning Dora away from her husband but I didn't care what it was. I picked up my purse and was about to leave when Annabelle stopped me.

"Jackie, I need to have a word with you alone, okay?"

Craig came around the table and gave me a kiss on the cheek. "Thanks for everything, Jackie. I'll remember you on the acknowledgments page." And then he was gone.

The acknowledgments page! Jesus! There had to be a polite way to discourage him from doing that.

"Sit down, Jackie." Annabelle gave me a generous smile. "Would you like some more juice?"

I declined.

"Jackie, as you know, the executive editor spot at Welburn Books has been open since Casey Esau left a few months ago."

Yes! Here it was. I was about to be promoted!

"It has been difficult for me to make a decision. You and Astrid Norstromm are both incredibly talented editors who work very hard. However, my decision is to be announced tomorrow at the editorial meeting but I wanted you to hear it from me first." She hesitated and looked down at her hands and I knew before she said it. "I have decided to promote Astrid because she works in a wider variety of categories."

Astrid Norstromm was a white woman and, like me, she edited all types of fiction and nonfiction. The only difference was that all her authors were white. Mine were all black.

Annabelle waited for me to say something, but I didn't dare open my mouth. There was no way for me to control what would come out of it and Mama's rent still had to be paid.

"I know you're disappointed, Jackie."

When she stopped talking I was going to make my escape and head straight home and get back into bed.

"Please don't quit on me, Jackie. You're a valued member of the staff and I promise that you'll get a sweet raise during the next evaluation period."

Evaluations took place each June. Therefore, the "sweet raise" was six months away.

"Annabelle, I really have to be going now." I got up and stomped out of her apartment before she could say another word.

If I'd known that Annabelle had already decided to give Astrid the job, I would have held my ground and fought harder for Moms Mabley. Instead, I'd sold her out big-time and this knowledge stuck in my craw.

I took a cab back uptown, turned the ringers on my

phone to the OFF position, climbed into a nightgown even though it was barely dusk, and went to sleep.

Sometime later, I felt a presence in the room. Peering through the shadows, I realized it was a Black man, about six-feet-one, broad-shouldered and stark naked. My first instinct was to scream, and then I realized it was Victor.

He laughed and it was a deep, throaty sound. "Hey, Jackie, sorry I scared you."

"Baby, that's quite all right."

He smiled, revealing the strong white teeth with the gap in the front which I loved so much.

I could barely breathe.

He leaned over and kissed me on the lips and there was a long moment of silence as we locked eyes.

My hands reached up to caress his face and my fingers traced his wide forehead, the velvety smoothness of his skin, eyes, and nose.

"Victor," *I whispered.* "You don't know how long I've yearned for this night."

"I'll know real soon," *he replied,* "because you'll tell me in the song you're about to sing."

He slid easily between the sheets and turned me to face him.

Slowly, Victor began to touch my stomach through the nightgown. Gently his big, dark hands moved up to stroke my hefty breasts. Then with exasperating self-control, he moved back down to my thighs, parting them, teasing the flesh.

"Victor," *I arched my back, breathing his name softly over and over again.*

"Just relax, sweetheart."

Victor swayed over until he was on top of me. I could feel his erection against my pubic hair, yet he only tongue-kissed me while running his fingers through my long braids. His tongue tasted sweet.

I took hold of his erection and my hand went up and down, "Victor, I want you to rip my gown off."

He did and the way I sang put Aretha Franklin to shame.

5

WEIGHT WATCHERS?

Mama was getting thinner. I could feel it that Sunday when I hugged her and see it when she took the bag of fruit from my hand and walked away.

My childhood home was a shotgun-style apartment. This means that all the rooms are in a straight line. If you stand at the front door and pull a trigger, the bullet will go straight to the back of the place without hitting any walls or doors. It was real old-fashioned, and there was no privacy at all because you simply walked through each bedroom.

Mama had tried hanging curtains at the end of each room one time, but it just made our home look more depressing so she took them down. The old furniture was gone, replaced with semi-expensive beds, sofa and matching loveseat, and a warm wood kitchen set. I had refurnished the place during my first year at Welburn Books when I was finally making some decent money. The old linoleum was gone, too, and now the place had red carpet on all the floors except the kitchen, which was a dark green tile. Every one of the walls had pictures of me or me and Mama. It warmed Mama's home but the photos of myself as an ugly, buck-toothed young girl made me shudder.

I hung my coat up in the living room closet, dropped my purse and overnight case on the sofa, and followed her into the kitchen.

"Are you okay, Mama? That housedress looks like it's hanging off of you."

She put the bag on a countertop and started taking the oranges and grapes out of it. "I'm just fine. Me and Elvira joined Weight Watchers. I'm glad to see that it's workin'."

Elvira was her friend from across the hall. "Weight Watchers! Mama, you've always been thin as a rail!"

"Maybe so but that's the only new group down at the senior citizens' place and me and Elvira is tired of just each other's company." She said this with a laugh. "We need some new blood."

I didn't believe Mama and made a mental note to get to the bottom of whatever was really going on. "Whatever happened to Bingo night at the local church for old ladies?"

She put the last of the fruit in the refrigerator. "Who you callin' an old lady?"

She was only pretending to be mad.

"We're tired of losing money at Bingo, so this is something different."

"Well, all right then, but don't get carried away."

I followed her out of the kitchen, down the hall, and into her bedroom, where she took her customary seat in an ancient, white, overstuffed armchair. Mama had settled into a pattern of loneliness. When Elvira wasn't around, she concentrated on a regular set of television programs with almost religious intensity. When I came over, it usually took her an hour or more to completely shift her focus onto my presence. I decided to use a few minutes of that time to call Alyssa.

"It ain't me that you should be worried about, Jacqueline. You're thirty-two years old and ain't got no man that I can see. I still can't figure out why you give Paul such a hard way to go when anybody with eyes can see he is crazy about you. If you don't wanna end up all alone like me, you better get busy."

No, I didn't have a man and nasty sex dreams involving me and Victor didn't count, although I had been smiling about last night's episode all the way downtown.

"I'm working on it, Mama."

"Good. I'd like to get a peek at a grandbaby before they put me in my casket."

Mama had been talking about that casket and planning her funeral ever since I could remember. The details were seared into my brain: Her sisters from Memphis were to be seated in the back of the church behind her friends because they'd never bothered to get on a train and come see her; the choir had to sing "Jesus Keep Me Near the Cross," and under no circumstances were they allowed to chirp one note of "Amazing Grace" because it was a song she detested; her casket was to be pink, not white; the dress she spent eternity in could not have one of those collars that went up to her chin and it had to be blue because it was a color that had always flattered her; most importantly, if my daddy showed up, I was to slap him silly.

I rubbed her short, gray hair and changed the subject before she could start reciting the grim details of her send-off once more. "What are you watching?"

The TV set was on and the volume was almost deafening, as usual.

"An old rerun of *Columbo*. The one where Johnny Cash murders his nagging wife."

That episode was my all-time favorite *Columbo*. "I've got to make a phone call and then I'll watch it with you."

"Okay," she replied, and then stared fixedly at the TV screen.

I used the kitchen phone to call Alyssa.

"Hello?"

"May I speak with Alyssa, please?"

"This is she."

"Alyssa, it's Jackie Blue. Are you all right?"

"I'm hanging in there, Jackie."

"Paul gave me your number. I hope you don't mind."

"No. It's kind of you to call."

"I'm really sorry about what happened, Alyssa."

"Thanks. I feel badly for Davina. She was really psyched about the project."

I didn't tell Alyssa that Elaine Garner had already stepped in to fill her shoes.

"Is there anything I can do?"

She laughed. "Do you know anyone who needs an editor?"

I thought for a moment. "Not offhand, but I'll keep my ears open."

She sighed. "Okay."

I had a sudden brainstorm. "Alyssa, I've got piles of unread manuscripts in my office right now. Do you want a couple of freelance jobs until you find something?"

"Love to!"

"Good. Let me pull some stuff together and I'll call you on Tuesday."

"Jackie, don't get into trouble on my account."

"What are you talking about?

"Marlene Rashker fucked up big-time, so she is covering her ass. I've heard some strange lies about myself over the past few days. Don't get tainted with my brush."

I was curious. "Are you going to sue them?"

"My parents want me to but I really shouldn't have blurted out Davina's instructions in the meeting that way. I could have told Marlene in private."

"And without witnesses, she would have taken that project away from you."

"You're right, but I really don't want to get tied up in some big, legal circus."

"Well, don't worry about me, Alyssa. I am going to help you regardless of what anyone thinks."

"What about the rest of the Black Pack?"

"They're running so hard for cover, they might pass the ghost of Jesse Owens on the way," I replied.

We both laughed and then I went back to rejoin my mother.

For the next two hours we watched the beleaguered singer struggle to be free of the wily, relentless detective.

It wasn't until after Lieutenant Columbo discovered the crucial piece of evidence that would hang his prey, Johnny Cash accepted his impending doom with remarkable grace, and the credits started to roll that I started telling Mama about the afternoon I'd spent with the Murrays.

She made a "humph" noise and got up. "Sounds like the husband's got a real nice hustle goin' for hisself. He plays aroun' with pens and pencils while she brings in the butter. What kinda sorry-ass man is that?"

Mama's kitchen was large. There was enough room for two people to move around in comfortably. I sat down at the round kitchen table that had been there since I was a child.

I chuckled at her dead-on portrait of Craig. "He is a man who doesn't see any reason why he should work when his wife's family owns a company that nets at least twenty million dollars a year. Even if he did go and get a nine-to-five, whatever he brought in would look like nothing. I guess he figures, why bother?"

"Do she boss him aroun'?"

"She didn't used to, but it looks like that is changing. Is there anything in this house to drink, Mama?"

She was cutting up the chicken. I could see the strain on her face as she pulled and tugged.

"You mean liquor?"

"Yeah."

"Nope. Me and Elvira drank the last li'l bit of rum night before las'."

"I thought y'all were supposed to be dieting," I teased.

"Dieting, baby, not dying."

I kicked off my shoes and shuffled to the refrigerator in my sweat socks. There wasn't much in the liquid department: a pitcher of water, a pitcher of red Kool-Aid, and one lone can of beer.

"Annabelle was sure wearing the pants in that house yesterday." I told her about the scene with Dora.

"So he can't even know what's wrong wit his own chile?"

"Looks that way," I agreed, and chugged half the beer before sitting back down.

"Well, it ain't your problem. Did your work go all right?"

"Let's just say that Moms Mabley is about to die all over again. Craig is . . . oh, never mind. I really don't want to rehash the whole thing. It's just too sad for Black folk."

She pulled at the breast of the chicken. "Did you keep your tongue at the bottom of your mouth?"

"Yeah, and I don't feel good about selling out like that."

"Someday we won't have to, baby."

"If you say so, Mama. By the way, it looks to me like you need a new set of sharp knives."

"I can make do with these for a while longer."

"No way. You're going to give yourself a nasty cut real soon. I'll make a note in my Filofax to drop by Blooming-dale's tomorrow evening."

"What's that?"

"What?"

"A Filowhatever."

"An organizing system in book form with tabs for daily appointments, tax records, notes, various lists and stuff. Wait, I'll show it to you."

A search of my handbag, overnight case, and Kate Spade duffel bag yielded nothing. I racked my brain trying to remember the last time I'd seen it, and then it hit me.

"Oh, Mama! I left my Filofax in Annabelle's library. This is a disaster!"

"Jackie, Vietnam was a disaster. This is just bothersome," she responded dryly. "Pick up the phone and call her. She can bring it to you tomorrow."

I slumped onto the sofa and started rocking back and forth. "What if she reads it? Aw man, Annabelle will know all my personal business."

"What kinda stuff did you write down in a book that anybody could get a hold of?"

"Everything, Mama," I explained that Filofax had the dates my menstrual periods started and ended on the calendar sheets, nasty comments about various people in the industry on the diary pages, affirmations designed to help me keep my temper in check at the Monday editorial meetings, childish sketches of hearts with my name entwined with Victor's in the middle of them, cleaner's tickets, laundry receipts, recent cancelled checks, and . . . oh God in heaven, all my notes relating to the Moms Mabley project . . . the things I'd said about Annabelle's husband!

By the time I finished, Mama was standing in the middle of the living room floor with her mouth hanging open. "I thought you had betta sense than this."

"Mama, I have to call Annabelle right now so she can find it before the cleaning lady throws it away or something." I headed for the phone.

"No! Don't call her!"

"But, you just said . . ." I spluttered.

"If you call her on a Sunday afternoon, she'll have time to find it and read it. Why don't you give her a ring tomorrow morning before she leaves for work and tell her you're droppin' by to pick it up. She'll be so busy runnin' aroun' gettin' her li'l girl dressed and pullin' her own self together for work that she won't have time to wonder what's in it."

I bit my lip. What Mama said made sense. But how was I going to sleep, knowing that it was in the Murrays' possession?

6

ANNABELLE AND THE
FILOFAX

The next morning I was so determined not to let Annabelle know my Filofax was in her house that I didn't even call ahead to let her know I was coming. The doorman in the lobby of Annabelle's building called upstairs and then waved me on inside.

The door opened on the eighth floor and Annabelle was standing in her vestibule, waiting for me. She was wearing a navy blue pantsuit, a pearl necklace with matching earrings, and black pumps. Her face was flushed, the forehead creased in a frown, the eyes red-rimmed. It was clear that she had been weeping. Had she and Craig been fighting? She crossed her arms across her chest and fixed me with a what-the-hell-are-you-doing-here stare.

My voice came out squeaky. "Good morning, Annabelle. I'm sorry to bother you so early in the morning, but I just realized that I left my Filofax in your library on Saturday."

She blinked twice. "Oh, is that all?"

What had she expected?

"Yes," I chuckled insincerely. "I have no idea what my

appointments are for the day. Isn't it amazing how missing one item can louse up your whole schedule?"

"Wait right here," she said shortly.

I waited, hoping that she wouldn't mention my show of ire the last time we were together.

She was back with the book in less than a minute. "Here you are," she said, thrusting it toward my chest. "Are you feeling better?"

What a dumb-assed question.

I seized the book, wondering if she had read it. "Yes, I'm very well this morning, thank you."

Her eyes met mine and she smiled. "Good. I'm glad we're friends again."

Friends?

A long time ago, Paul and I had discussed quitting our jobs and opening our own publishing house. We had become discouraged when research indicated that we needed at least one million dollars to get the project off the ground. It was time for us to sit down and talk about it again. In the meantime, if Annabelle wanted to believe that I wasn't pissed off to the bone, that was fine with me. I smiled back at her and got back into the elevator. Before the door closed, I waved and said, "See you at the office."

She waved back and her expression was so innocent that it was clear she had not been aware of the appointment book before my visit. I opened it and gasped. Jamal Hunt was due in my office in five minutes. When the elevator door opened, I broke into a run, straight past the startled doorman and out onto the street, where I waved frantically for a cab.

The driver chose to go down Columbus Avenue, and I didn't notice it until we were smack-dab in a bumper-to-bumper, rush-hour traffic jam. After haranguing the driver to no avail and racing through my building's security checkpoint, I vaulted into the reception area of Welburn Books, looking breathless and agitated.

I recognized Jamal Hunt immediately, even though his author photo hardly came close to doing him justice. He was a young man in his mid-twenties with a bronze complexion, square jaw, high cheekbones, and, when he realized who I was, his full lips parted into a sexy grin. Jamal stood up and held out a hand for me to shake. He wore a dark brown suit, crisp white shirt, and a beige tie. I was a little puzzled because his outfit seemed at odds with the edgy, hip-hop fiction which had earned him such notoriety.

"Mr. Hunt, I apologize for keeping you waiting. I was stuck in a traffic jam."

"Apology accepted, Miss Blue," he replied smoothly. His voice rumbled like a bass drum. He picked up his coat and briefcase to follow me through the beige-carpeted corridors, which were already buzzing with office-type activity. He looked at the gilt-framed portraits of long dead Welburns that lined the ivory walls. "Who are these folk?"

"My boss's ancestors. Welburn Books is a family-owned firm."

He whistled. "They must have major dollars."

I smiled and waved him into my office.

We were just settling down when my assistant, Asha, appeared in the doorway. "Good morning, Jackie. I'm going to the cafeteria. Do you want anything?" She was a tiny young woman whom I had hired straight out of Hampton University two years ago. She had a pretty, heart-shaped face and wore her shoulder-length hair in dreadlocks. I made the introductions; she sucked in her stomach and thrust out her chest when Jamal turned that megawatt smile on her.

"Would you like some coffee or tea, Mr. Hunt?" I asked.

"No, but thank you—and please call me Jamal."

Asha left, closing the door behind her.

Even though Dallas had cautioned me that dealing with Jamal would not be easy, I had not dwelled on it. Most novelists were lonely people who lived inside their heads, and, like many editors, I knew that the best way to deal with them was just to listen when they were suffering from writer's block or needed to kvetch because their books had not set the world on fire. I was kind and patient with all my authors—those whose books were sinking into oblivion were treated exactly the same as those whose books were flying out of the stores.

A new relationship with an author always held the prospect of lifelong friendship. Jamal waited for me to wade into the waters of getting-to-know-you small talk. I encouraged him to talk about how he handled the writing process and then launched into some funny stories that other writers had told me about things they had done in an effort to cure writer's block.

He sat with his legs wide open, the way young men in their twenties seemed to do these days, and used his hands a lot to make his points.

Jamal chuckled a few times and then abruptly changed the topic to what was really on his mind. "What has Dallas Mowrey told you about me?"

"Not a whole lot," I answered carefully.

"Somebody told me that she goes around saying she does the writing for me."

This conversation could quickly degenerate into petty he said, she said bullshit and my in-box was stacked with work that needed my attention. "Jamal," I said firmly, "let's use this time to discuss taking your career to the next level."

"Fine. Exactly how much advertising, publicity, and promotion money is Welburn going to invest in my next book?"

Gulp. "I really don't know the exact amount, Jamal. However, I will say that we will mount an aggressive campaign to get the word out about it."

He waved away my bureaucratic piddle-paddle with a languid gesture of the wrist that made me smile. "Stop. Please. Why don't I tell you the plot of the book and you let me know what you think?" Jamal spent the next half hour walking me through a thriller involving race, robbery, deceit, and espionage set in the world of 1980s hip-hop that was absolutely Byzantine in its complexity.

"So," he concluded, "do you think *A Time to Chill* will be a best seller?"

All of Jamal's books were best-sellers because he was a shameless media hound who made sure that every publication, no matter how small, knew about the work he was doing.

Before I could answer, Asha opened the door without knocking. "I'm sorry, Jackie, but the editorial meeting is about to start."

Jamal glanced at his watch and stood up. "I've taken up enough of your time. Thanks for seeing me, Jackie. I look forward to working with you."

I bid him adieu and shook his hand. "Asha will show you to the elevators."

The door was now wide open and I could see my colleagues filing past, clutching manuscripts, notes, and books. I grabbed my stack of projects and joined them.

Leigh Dafoe, our editorial director, was already seated at the head of the conference room table, waiting for us to take our seats. Like the other members of the Black Pack, I was the only African-American at the table.

The way editorial meetings work is this: all of the editors sit at the table; there are chairs around the wall for the editorial assistants, publicists, and other marketing personnel. Leigh went around the table, giving each editor a chance to talk about the manuscripts they wanted to buy. There were ten of us at the table, and given the fact that all of us had a stack of papers, it looked like the session would last at least two hours.

Astrid Norstromm, the pasty-faced, stringy-haired white woman who was due to get the job I wanted, sat as close to Leigh as possible. She always did that—I guessed it was to remind the rest of us that the two women were close, personal friends. Astrid had no ass, no tits, buck teeth, and freckles. Yet she carried herself in a regal manner—almost as if she looked in the mirror every morning and saw the late Princess Diana staring back. Astrid had been hired to acquire and edit literary nonfiction for the company and had "a very big interest in Black people." She was constantly either in my office trying to get me excited about some project that would be of absolutely no interest to African-American book buyers or tying up the editorial meeting for long, agonizing minutes while she stumbled and stammered her way through book ideas about Black life that were so ridiculously off the mark that they would be laughable if it didn't happen so often.

I smiled at everyone except Astrid as I sat down.

Leigh started us off by announcing that she had purchased the American publishing rights to a first novel by a young British woman. The story was a love triangle set in the Victorian era.

Astrid was next. She tucked her thin, mousy brown hair behind her ears and flashed everyone a smile. "I've received a couple of terrific manuscripts over the past week." She spoke in a whispery voice that made us all strain to hear her and had a habit of placing her hands delicately in the center of her flat chest when she got excited. We were supposed to believe that too much emotion would send her into a fit of the vapors. Her whole presentation was straight-up Melanie Wilkes from

Gone With the Wind, and it made the other women at the table exchange angry glances whenever we could get away with it.

"The first one," she breathed, "is a fictionalized version of Harriet Tubman's life that I'm hoping Jackie will take a look at. The author is a history professor at Vassar and she has done extensive research in this area. I really love this project because the professor's writing is so vivid and colorful that you feel like you are really sitting in the Tubman cabin watching the events unfold." Astrid paused, her hands went to her chest, and she fastened her blue-eyed gaze briefly on each one of us. "I learned so much! Most people don't realize that the people in those slave cabins were not just workers. They were real families and behaved like genuine human beings."

I tried not to sound angry. "Real families? Genuine human beings?"

"Yes. Most people don't see the slaves in that light. Can you read it overnight?"

I ignored the question. "Is there any other news in the book . . . besides the announcement that Harriet Tubman and her family were genuine human beings?"

She seemed delighted at my interest. "Yes. The author is a feminist and she takes a look at the misogyny that was rampant among Black men in the slave quarters."

Pam Silberstein gasped and shot me a sympathetic look from across the table.

My throat was closing up and my next question (which I'd already guessed the answer to) squeaked out between my clenched teeth. "Is the author African-American?"

The stupid fool finally realized that the room was silent and something was very, very wrong. She looked at Leigh Dafoe for help. "The author is white. Does that make a difference?"

Leigh looked very uncomfortable. "Of course it doesn't. I'm sure Jackie was just trying to get an overall sense of this book. Do you have anything else to share with us?"

I glared at Astrid. She glared back.

"No. That's it for me but I'd like to make a generous offer on this project and we'll have to move quickly. The agent already has interest."

"We'll talk about it later," Leigh answered smoothly.

We all breathed a sigh of relief as the romance editor launched into a tale of the search for Mr. Right set on the French Riviera.

And then it was my turn. But before I could speak, Leigh's assistant rushed in and whispered something in her ear. Whatever it was caused Leigh to turn ashen and rush from the room without a word.

We gossiped and chitchatted among ourselves for almost twenty minutes.

By the time Leigh came back, we were beginning to run out of small talk.

Leigh's face was completely devoid of color. She looked somber. Just as our rustling and whispering stopped, Leigh burst into tears. "I don't know how to say this . . . it's just too awful," she said.

Astrid patted her on the back. "What's wrong?"

"I'm . . . um . . . all right," Leigh sniffled and stuttered. "There is . . . um . . . no easy um . . . way to . . . um . . . say this. . . . Annabelle Welburn . . . um, oh, God . . . has been murdered!"

7

I'M NOT LOOKING FOR THAT

Cries of grief, dismay, and disbelief ripped through the crowd but I was too astonished to react in any way until I saw Pamela Silberstein sag in her chair with tears running down her face. Although I had friendly relationships with all my colleagues with the exception of Astrid Norstromm, Pam was my hands-down favorite person on the staff. She was a tall white woman in her mid-fifties with shocking red hair and a razor-sharp wit who had been in charge of the health books for the past two decades.

I managed to reach her on legs that felt wobbly. I leaned down and asked the same stupid question that one always asks in these situations. "Are you all right?"

She looked up at me, her green eyes filled with pain, and said, "Never felt better, Jackie. How about you?"

How about me? It had been fourteen years since I'd received such stunning news. During the summer between high school and college a neighborhood girl named Carmen Rivera had been thrown from the roof of a dinky hotel over on 46th Street. According to pedestrians, Carmen screamed as she fell and then pretty much exploded when she hit the unyielding concrete. Her boyfriend was on the roof with her when it happened but, even though the Rivera family pressed the police to arrest him, nothing was done because he said they'd been sniffing cocaine together and she lost her balance. Carmen was known to dabble in drugs and there was no one left to contradict his story, so he went free.

Would Annabelle Murray's killer also get away with the crime?

Carmen had been a sweet, peaceful girl who had shared her candy necklace with me one day in kindergarten. Although we weren't friends after elementary school, her terrible death left me feeling miserable and wracked with pain, long after the funeral was over.

What were we supposed to do now?

Leigh asked us not to talk to the media and said we could go home if we felt like it.

Pam rose from her chair, we hugged briefly, and then, like cattle in a herd, followed our stricken colleagues out of the room.

I parked myself in Pam's office, which was so crammed with manuscripts and books that it usually made me claustrophobic after five minutes. Today was different. I was too traumatized to care about the untidiness surrounding me. It seemed impossible that Annabelle was not going to pop in on the marketing meeting that afternoon, lead the pre-sales conferences next week, secure a publishing deal for Craig, give me the raise, or . . .

"Poor little girl," I said aloud.

Pam's head was resting on her hand. "Dora?"

"Yes, life is hard enough without losing your mother."

"What in the world happened?" Pam sighed.

"When I saw Annabelle this morning, she was already dressed for work. Maybe she got mugged outside the park. She would definitely have resisted if someone tried to snatch her bag."

"You saw Annabelle this morning?"

Uh-oh. Annabelle had sworn me to secrecy on the Moms Mabley project and I wasn't about to betray her trust, especially now. "Yes, I was campaigning for a promotion."

Pam's eyes were riveted on me. "Oh, my God! Where was she? How did she look?"

I told her what Annabelle had been wearing and that I'd seen her at The Dakota but omitted the fact that she looked as though she'd been crying.

It was time for me to leave before I ended up putting Annabelle's business in the street. I stood up. "Pam, I'll see you later. Are you going to be okay?"

Her green eyes welled up with tears again and she nodded.

On the way back to my office I noticed that the atmosphere was hushed and dismal, although there were several knots of assistants standing around whispering about how the crime might have happened. The junior staff had very little contact with the head honchos like Annabelle and Leigh, so they really couldn't be expected to mourn.

On impulse, I walked into the bullpen-like area where Asha spent her working hours. She was on the phone but hung up immediately when she saw me approaching her desk. Asha's face looked just a little sad and confused.

"Do I have any messages?"

She handed me a stack of pink slips.

I leafed through them quickly: Penelope Aaron, a few writers, and Alyssa.

My line rang again while I was standing there. Asha put the caller on hold. "It's Paul," she said.

"I'll take it in my office." In my disoriented state, a chat with a trusted friend would provide a tiny bit of relief.

"I guess you heard about what happened," I managed to say before bursting into tears.

"No. I was just calling to chat. Why are you crying?" He paused for a moment. "Jackie, what's wrong? Did Victor get married or something?"

Perish the thought. "Paul, somebody killed my boss this morning." The words clogged up my throat and the tears continued to slide down my face.

He gasped. "That's terrible! I just ran into her at a cocktail party last week. She told me she had just booked a cruise to Bermuda."

"I'm not talking about Leigh. I meant Annabelle."

"Jesus Christ! What the hell happened?"

"If Leigh knows anything, she's not saying." I filled him in on the morning's events and then weariness overtook me. "Paul, I'm going to grab some manuscripts to read and go home."

Penelope Aaron called while I was packing to leave.

"Hey, girl, a great proposal came in yesterday. I figured a shout out to you was what time it is."

Penelope did not know how stupid she sounded and the shock of Annabelle's death had left me too wiped out to say anything.

"Tell me about it," I said wearily.

"Is something wrong, Jackie?"

"Yes, but I don't want to discuss it."

Penelope and everyone else would find out about the tragedy soon enough.

"Maybe I should holla at you tomorrow."

"No, go ahead."

She plunged right in. "It's called *Hell on Wheels* and it's a memoir by an ex-gang leader out of Los Angeles. He really gives up the goods. There is murder, rape, extortion, and shady dealings with the police department. Fascinating stuff. I'm telling you, Jackie, it has bestseller written all over it."

It was the type of book I hated but Penelope was right about the sales potential. For some reason, tales of Black degradation and depravity usually did extremely well at the cash register and my superiors would chop my head off if I didn't at least consider it.

"Sure, I'll take a look."

"Great! I'll messenger it right over."

"Fine."

"Hang in there, chile."

" 'Bye, Penelope."

It was noon when I stepped out of the building. It seemed strange to see the whole world marching on as though no tragedy had occurred.

To make matters worse, there was an e-mail waiting for me at home. It said

Jackie:
    I have my hands full with my girlfriend and career. Thank you for the offer but I'm not looking for THAT.
    If you have any business-related requests, I will help you if I can.
    Victor

THAT. He had referred to the most precious part of my body as a THAT . . . like it was an old piece of liver, not fit for human consumption. It felt like someone had kicked me in the stomach with a steel-toed boot and, like a fool, I wrote him back and told him so. Now I had no dignity either.

8

BAD NEWS

I tossed and turned all night and woke up feeling exhausted. It was nine o'clock, which meant Richard's Soul Food Diner was open for breakfast. After a quick shower, I slid into a black knit dress with a cowl neck and knee-length black boots. It was freezing outside and as I turned the corner onto 112th Street, a blast of cold wind hit me in the face, forcing my head down to my chest. The little Spanish man who sold newspapers next to the subway station was doing a brisk business. I paid for *The New York Times*, the *New York Daily News*, and the *New York Comet*.

A smiling photo of Annabelle was on the cover of each.

It was only a two-minute walk from the newspaper guy to Richard's Soul Food Diner. He was sitting at the counter watching his customers eat and his face lit up when I came through the door. I gave him a quick kiss and climbed onto the next stool.

"Jackie, I was just thinking about you. Did you know that woman who was killed yesterday morning?"

"Richard, it was my boss who was killed."

His jaw dropped. "The one you went to see on Saturday?"

"Yes. It's awful. I'm surprised Paul didn't tell you."

"He called me yesterday but this place was so crowded, I didn't have time to talk. I heard about the murder on the radio this morning and when they said she worked in book publishing, I figured you might know her, but damn, I never expected this."

"Richard, I really want to take a look at the papers," I answered impatiently.

"Yeah . . . sure . . . are you hungry?"

It had been more than twenty-four hours since I'd last had anything to eat. I ordered pancakes and orange juice and opened the *Comet*. Richard yelled my request to his cook, seized the *News*, and we buried ourselves in stories of Annabelle's life and premature death.

PUBLISHING EXECUTIVE FOUND STRANGLED, read the *Comet* headline. The paper reported that Annabelle Welburn Murray, publisher of Welburn Books and daughter of the late John Welburn who had inherited the illustrious publishing house from his parents thirty years before, was strangled sometime before nine-thirty Monday morning. Her sister, noted Park Avenue decorator Sarah Jane Welburn, discovered the body, fully clothed, in a bathroom of the sumptuous penthouse. "There were signs of a desperate struggle and Mrs. Murray fought hard for her life," Detective Marcus Gilchrist of the NYPD was quoted as saying.

The story went on to say that there was no sign of forced entry and police had no suspects.

My hands were shaking so badly, the newspaper fluttered to the floor. Up until then, I had assumed that Annabelle was attacked on her way to work, but now it seemed that the killer had struck only minutes after I left her apartment. If I had stayed just a little longer, there might have been two dead bodies in the morgue right now instead of one.

Richard caught me just as the room began to sway.

9

GOOD-BYE

The torrent of media interest, which accompanies any murder of someone rich or famous, overwhelmed the staff of Welburn Books. Our offices were flooded with calls and e-mails from journalists, television producers, a couple of film companies, and radio news directors. When members of the Black Pack called, I gave them what little information I had, but each representative of the media who managed to get me on the phone only received a terse "no comment" for their trouble.

It was only natural that the workers began to panic once the initial shock of Annabelle's death wore off. Pam Silberstein popped in one afternoon wearing a crisp navy blue suit and black pumps. She closed the door behind her and plopped down into a chair. "I've just come from my first job interview in more than twenty years. It was arduous."

"Where did you interview?"

"Can't tell you that, kiddo, but I suggest you get moving, too."

I shrugged. "One of the other Welburns will take Annabelle's place."

"I doubt that. When her father died, she was the only one who had any interest in the company. The Welburns will sell it."

After that conversation, I told Paul to start leaking the word that I might be available to speak with interested parties. The week went by so fast that I didn't have too much time to obsess over Victor's disinterest in fondling the most precious part of my body—the part he had so callously referred to as THAT.

Since Annabelle had come to such a terrible end, it was very selfish of me to worry about how the tragedy would affect my own life or career. I should call Craig and ask if he needed me to help him in any way. My feelings about his book weren't important. He had loved his wife and now had to bury her and raise their bewildered and heartbroken child alone. But every time I called, someone would answer and say that he was not home or too grief-stricken to come to the phone. One morning I turned on the TV while I was getting dressed for work. A stony-faced newscaster said

> *"Police are still investigating the murder of Annabelle Welburn Murray at her luxurious apartment in The Dakota last Monday morning.*
> *Dakota residents interviewed say that they have not seen any suspicious activity in or around the building and officials admit that they have no leads. However, police are reviewing video surveillance tapes of the area."*

Annabelle's funeral was held the following Tuesday at the Frank E. Campbell Funeral Chapel on Madison Avenue. According to the morning newscast, a veritable Who's Who of American industry were expected to be among the mourners.

Four gigantic bunches of pink roses surrounded the altar which held Annabelle's closed white casket. Every seat in the place was filled with her family and friends, leaving the Welburn employees to stand in the back.

I was flanked by Pam and Astrid. The three of us wept softly throughout the short service. Annabelle had been a good person and she didn't deserve to come to such a horrible end. As the tears poured down my cheeks, I wished fervently that whoever murdered her was caught by sundown and electrocuted by morning.

There was only one eulogy, given by a distinguished-looking, elderly gentleman who spoke succinctly yet with feeling about Annabelle's life and the sorrow that now held her family captive. As a soloist burst into what sounded like an aria, I glimpsed another Black face in the room. It was Victor. I twisted and turned to get a better look until Pam gave me a disapproving glance.

Another musical selection followed, and then it was over.

We all filed somberly out of Frank E. Campbell's, and into the media frenzy. As we fought our way past the camera crews, I saw that Victor had somehow worked his way up to the front of the mob. What was he doing there? I pushed and shoved my way through the crowd to ask him, but he was gone by the time I broke free.

A week after the funeral, Leigh Dafoe called another meeting to announce that Welburn Books was not going to be sold and our jobs were, for the most part, secure. Craig Murray was our new publisher and editor-in-chief. He would address his employees and take over his new duties as soon as the family's affairs were in order.

Visions of a truckload of horrible books aimed at African-American book buyers danced through my head and I left the meeting determined to land a new job before Craig took the reins.

10

DETECTIVE MARCUS GILCHRIST

Late one afternoon, I was busily updating my résumé when a tall, barrel-chested white man walked into my office without knocking. He had dark, nondescript hair, piercing brown eyes, and a bushy moustache. His overcoat was gray, and even though it was a frigid February day, he was not wearing gloves.

"Jacqueline Blue?"

"Yes?"

He held out a hand and I shook the icy appendage.

"May I sit down?"

He closed the door and sat down before I had a chance to answer.

"Miss Blue, I'm Detective Marcus Gilchrist from the NYPD. I'm meeting with all the senior staffers here regarding the murder of Annabelle Murray. Do you have a few moments?"

"Hold on a second." I closed the document and turned the computer monitor away so I could give him my undivided attention. "What can I do for you?"

"You may be able to help me catch a killer."

He waited for some response from me and I waited for him to go on.

"Miss Blue, are you aware that you are the last person to see Annabelle Welburn Murray alive?"

"What?"

He sighed and took a little notepad from his coat pocket. "I'm afraid it's true, ma'am. You did visit Miss Welburn on the morning that she died, correct?"

"Yes."

"Why don't you tell me about it?"

So I did.

"Hmmm—who else was in the apartment?"

"I don't know. I never went past the vestibule."

"And you say her eyes were red-rimmed?"

"Yes. I'm sure she'd just finished crying."

"Then what happened?"

"I got back in the elevator and went to work."

"Were you in a hurry?"

"No."

Wrong answer. Detective Gilchrist sat up straight and closed the notebook with a snap. "Yes, you were."

"What?"

"There is a video surveillance camera in the lobby of that apartment building, Miss Blue. Were you aware of that?"

"No."

His mouth smiled. His eyes most certainly did not. "I didn't think so. I have a videotape that shows you running through the lobby toward the exit. It sure looks like you were in a hurry."

And then I remembered Jamal. "Yes, you're right. I realized that I was late for an appointment with an author."

"I see." He stroked his moustache for a moment without taking his eyes off my face.

Detective Marcus Gilchrist was trying to scare me and I didn't like it. "Is that all, Detective?"

"Can you think of anyone who wanted to harm Mrs. Murray?"

"No."

"Do you have any information that may be helpful to us in catching her killer?"

"No."

"Did you like your boss, Miss Blue?"

"Yes."

"Mrs. Welburn told her husband that you left their apartment in quite a huff the previous Saturday . . . something about a promotion you were expecting?"

Oh Jesus, help me. I chose my words carefully. "Annabelle and I had discussed the possibility of my taking on some new duties. I was a little disappointed, that's all."

"I'm going to need you to come uptown and give us a statement, Miss Blue, and I'll tell you why."

He leaned over the desk so far that our noses were practically touching. "According to what you've just told me, you showed up at Mrs. Welburn's apartment unannounced, she let you into her home, you tore through that lobby like a bat outta hell, and her sister came along only fifteen minutes later to find her sibling strangled in her own ladies' room."

The editor in me wanted to correct him. The term "ladies' room" was incorrect in this instance since the facilities were used by men as well.

"Do you know why this story bothers me, Miss Blue?"

I pressed my lips together and said nothing.

"It bothers me because between the time you left the building and Mrs. Welburn's sister entered it, no one else came in or out." He reached into his coat pocket and pulled out a videotape cassette. "I have the videotape, Miss Blue. No delivery men, no maids, no butlers. No one."

By this time, I was shaking so hard, I had to hold on to the seat of my chair.

"I'm sure you can see why I need a written statement from you, right?"

"I did not kill my boss, and I'm not talking to you anymore until someone finds me a lawyer."

Detective Marcus Gilchrist rose slowly from the chair and walked to the door. He paused with his hand on the knob. "You have exactly twenty-four hours to appear at the precinct, Miss Blue."

When the door closed behind him, I phoned Paul.

II

WINNER

As a criminal defense lawyer to the stars, Keith Williams was unsurpassed in his field. It was he, for instance, who saved a white soap opera star, Clarise Buchanan, from death by legal injection for allegedly killing her mother. He had also won an acquittal for Lawbreaker, the Grammy Award-winning rapper, after a long and costly trial. Several eyewitnesses testified that they saw Lawbreaker beat his valet with a baseball bat for trash-talking him. The servant died several hours later from his injuries, but the jury believed Keith, who told them that the valet had been complaining of excruciating headaches for several weeks before the beating and that his death could have been caused by an aneurysm. I was well aware of Williams's reputation—that he was a shark, but in a way that had earned him the respect of his peers. He was a smooth operator who left no stone unturned in his pursuit of reasonable doubt.

As Keith Williams recalled in his appropriately titled 1995 autobiography, *Winner,* which Paul Dodson edited, *I decided during my first year out of law school that "not guilty" was the only verdict I would ever accept.*

Paul listened to my story. "I'm calling Keith Williams," he said grimly.

The two men had become good friends during the two years it took for them to pull Keith's book together.

"Isn't that rather like using a machine gun to kill a cockroach?"

"I'm not going to ask him to go to the precinct with you personally, but there are a lot of hungry young lawyers in his office. Maybe he'll send one of them as a favor to me."

"It can't hurt to ask," I agreed.

"I'll call you right back."

It took half an hour and seemed like six months. I tried to read but couldn't concentrate. My hand reached for the receiver to call Mama but she was already upset enough about how close I had come to meeting a homicidal maniac. So I surfed the net—reading celebrity news, my horoscope, which said that I should watch my spending, and online reviews of several books I had worked on. By the time Paul called back, I had bitten the inside of my cheek until it hurt.

"Keith wants you to get in a cab and come over to his office right now."

"What? How much will he charge me for this?"

"Jackie, listen to me. There is a rich, powerful white woman lying under six feet of dirt, victim of a homicide, and nobody is in jail for it. The police have everyone from the mayor to the president screaming for justice. Quick justice. That videotape of you running across the lobby is no joke, and Keith says someone will leak it to the media before the weekend. I didn't ask Keith how much money he wants because right now I just don't care."

This was crazy talk as far as I was concerned. "Paul, that detective did scare me. But now that I think about it, maybe his job is to scare everyone who Annabelle ever met until he finds the criminal."

"What about the videotape?" Paul asked quietly.

"He isn't stupid enough to arrest me just for running across a lobby."

"By the way, Jackie, did Annabelle ever get back to you about the position you wanted?"

My throat closed.

"Jackie, are you still there?"

"She turned me down, Paul. She decided to promote Astrid Norstromm. It was to be announced on the day she was murdered."

Paul didn't say anything else. There was no need to.

12

TRUMP

His office was located in Trump Tower on Fifth Avenue. The reception area was decorated in muted beige and burgundy and a classy-looking Black woman with a plastic smile sat at the front desk. She used a pencil to push numbers on the telephone console and spoke to someone after I gave her my name. "His secretary will be with you in a moment," she told me.

I took a seat in a burgundy chair and started leafing impatiently through an *Upscale* magazine that lay on a circular chrome table.

A few minutes later, a door opened behind me and I turned to face a petite little thing, about my age, who could probably fit into a size two dress. Her skin was the color of a hazelnut. She had delicate cheekbones, short dreadlocks which she wore tied up in a rubber band, and deep-set brown eyes. Her black knit pantsuit was cut smartly and matched her swank surroundings.

"Hello, I'm Debbie," she said. Please follow me."

We went down a long hallway that had offices on both sides and lots of earnest-looking men and women doing business in them. Finally, she led me into an enormous

room that had white walls and carpet with silver standing lamps and glass furniture. Awards and diplomas
hung on one wall and framed press clippings took up
most of another. B.B. King's "Paying the Cost to Be the
Boss," one of my favorite tunes, was playing softly on an
unseen music system.

I stood in the doorway staring at a man who spent so
much time on my television screen, I felt like I already
knew him. He was strikingly handsome.

Debbie introduced us.

I watched as Keith advanced toward me. His pace was
smooth, his pants fell meticulously over his shiny black
wing tip shoes, his gray suit jacket fit perfectly on his
muscular torso, and the elegant white shirt contrasted
nicely with his skin. If he has a girlfriend, she must spend
a lot of time worrying about the effect his looks and fame
have on other women, I thought.

He extended his hand. "Pleased to meet you, Miss
Blue."

"Thank you," I replied, unable to take my eyes off him.

He was a handsome man, over six feet tall, broad-
shouldered and muscular. His skin was the color of but-
terscotch with a spoonful of cream; the eyes were dark
and probing. He carried himself in a sturdy, confident
manner.

"I really appreciate your seeing me, Mr. Williams."

"Please call me Keith."

The woman left us alone, closing the door behind
her.

"I love the blues," I said nervously.

"Have a seat," Keith said, indicating a burgundy visitor's chair which faced his desk.

I sat.

"Who is your favorite bluesman?" Keith asked, sitting
down in the plush white chair behind his glass desk,
which had lots of neat stacks of paper on it.

"Robert Johnson," I replied.

"Good choice. I haven't been able to make up my mind. Some days it's Blind Lemon Jefferson, then Bobby Bland. Today, it's B.B." He leaned back and smiled. "Well, Miss Blue, tell me how you got yourself into such a mess."

"Call me Jackie, okay?"

He nodded.

"I'm not really in a mess. I'm only here because this detective came to my job with a videotape that might be taken the wrong way. Plus, I have to go to the police station to make a statement and I'm scared."

He held up a hand. "Whoa. Start from the beginning. What were you doing in the victim's building?"

"I went there to get my appointment book. I'd left it in her apartment two days before."

"What were you doing in her apartment two days before?"

"Working on a book about Moms Mabley."

He chuckled. "Oh, yeah. Paul mentioned something like that when he called. What made you decide to do a book about her?"

"I didn't. Annabelle's husband was doing her life story. I was there to edit the project."

"Tell me everything."

I talked for fifteen minutes without stopping. Keith never took his eyes from my face. His expression was bland, so I couldn't tell whether he believed me or not. When I finished, he rubbed his chin thoughtfully and pressed a button on his telephone system.

A male voice came over the speakerphone. "Yes?"

Keith said, "I need you to look into a situation for me. It's not urgent but I don't want to get caught unprepared."

"What is the situation?"

"I have a young woman in my office who has stumbled into an unfortunate set of circumstances. Have you been keeping up with that story of the publishing executive who was strangled?"

The voice replied. "Did I have a choice? It's on every station. CNN ran a segment on it just last night."

"Good. I want you to find out everything there is to know about the victim and her husband. Where they were born, married, lived, who their friends were, who loved them, hated them. Get the picture?"

"Got it."

Keith released the button and swiveled around back to me.

"Who was that?" I asked.

"One of my best detectives."

I folded my hands in my lap to keep them from shaking. "How many do you have?"

"Six at last count."

"Who are all the other people milling around?"

He raised an eyebrow. "Why are you so interested?"

" 'Impressed' would be more accurate."

He chuckled. "I have a few lawyers and a couple of paralegals in addition to my research team. Can we get back to your problem, now?"

"Yes."

"If Annabelle Murray swore you to secrecy, why does Paul Dodson know about the project?"

"Paul and I are close personal friends. I knew he wouldn't say anything."

"You were wrong."

"What?"

"He told me, right?"

"Annabelle did not want anyone in book publishing to know what her husband was up to. I doubt that she would object to Paul telling a famous criminal lawyer anything he thought would help me stay out of some serious trouble."

He nodded. "Fine. I'm going with you to see this detective, and when we get there, you must follow my lead. Talk when I say it is okay. Stop talking when I say stop. I'll get a copy of the videotape and release it to the media myself."

"Why?"

He smiled enigmatically. "Trust me, Jackie."

"I'd rather not have the videotape released at all," I said, close to tears. "Isn't there something you can do to stop it?"

"No, and it is definitely not a good idea for me to try."

"This is going to make me look so bad."

"Bad?" He whirled around in his chair. "It doesn't have to. It all depends on the spin you put on it."

I wasn't in the mood for riddles. "How much are your services going to cost me?"

He shrugged. "Paul Dodson is a good friend of mine. I'm not going to charge you anything. Unless there is something you haven't told me, I predict that the cops will leave you alone after you give them a statement tonight."

I felt a whole better.

13

PAUL STILL WAITING

I didn't get home until ten that night so I missed yet
another Black Pack meeting. Paul was still up, waiting
for my phone call.

"What happened?"

"Keith went with me. You should have seen Detective
Gilchrist's face when I walked in with him. The man
practically genuflected."

Paul chuckled.

"He walked me through the morning Annabelle was
killed. Then I wrote it all down and left."

"So what happens now?"

"Keith is releasing the videotape to some reporter
friend of his tomorrow."

"Best offense is a good defense, huh?"

"Something like that."

"I know you are upset right now, Jackie, but there is
something I want to ask you when things settle down."

Oh no! I knew what the something was. He had been
waiting to ask it for a long time.

"Today has been rough, Paul. I can feel my brain
shutting down."

"I'm glad everything turned out okay, Jackie. I was worried."

I yawned. "I've got to call Mama and then get some sleep."

"Okay. Will you be home tomorrow?"

"No, I'm going to spend the day with Mama. She is still pretty frazzled about this whole thing. I need to reassure her that its almost over."

"Alyssa came to the Black Pack meeting tonight. She told us that you signed her up for a few projects."

"That's right."

"Maybe you should have waited to see what the fall-out will be for her."

In other words, wait until Alyssa got back on the white folks' good side before hugging her to our collective bosom again. It was some sad, gutless plantation-type thinking and I didn't want to talk about it.

I changed the subject and tried to sound casual. "Who else showed up tonight?"

"Yes, Victor was there," Paul said brusquely.

"I didn't ask."

"Whatever," he snapped.

"Good night, Paul," I said softly, "and thanks for Keith."

"Don't mention it." He hung up.

I hadn't told Paul about the insulting e-mail that Victor had sent me. Maybe it was because I was ashamed of being treated so badly. Or maybe I was afraid he'd say that I deserved it for throwing myself at Victor again.

In any case, with the detective coming to my office, riding downtown in the back of Keith Williams's limousine and the videotape, which would probably be aired Monday morning, I'd have quite a story to tell at Black Pack next week.

Maybe I could embellish it a little and make Victor believe that Keith Williams was romantically interested in me. That would make him kick his girlfriend and her pretty new underwear straight to the curb.

14

DUST

By Sunday night, I was running across Mama's television screen with my braids flying behind me as I glanced anxiously at my watch and shoved the appointment book into my bulging tote bag at the same time. The doorman watched my hasty exit from the building in open-mouthed surprise and the tape ended in a flurry of static. The scene changed and Keith Williams was standing in front of The Dakota apartment building, surrounded by strobe lights and microphones.

He looked straight into the cameras and spoke firmly. "It is a testament to Mrs. Murray's character that she inspired the kind of dedication from her workers evidenced by this videotape. My client, Jacqueline Blue, was rushing off to meet with famed novelist Jamal Hunt, who was waiting for her in the offices of Welburn Books."

Flurries of shouted questions were flung at him. *Why did Miss Blue hire you? What were Annabelle Murray's last words? How long had Miss Blue worked for the deceased?* Keith waited for silence and then continued with what was obviously a well-rehearsed speech. "Miss Blue is deeply distressed by the death of her employer, whom she held in extremely high regard. Like Mrs. Murray's family, she is hoping that the killer is brought to justice as quickly as possible. I have nothing more to say." He marched to his limousine with the reporters trailing him and shouting more questions. As the car drove away, the outdoor scene disappeared and the program went back to the studio.

Mama sighed. "What are you gonna do, Jackie?"

"There is nothing I can do except keep my head down and hope this all blows over real fast."

"Be careful, honey. This is a real dangerous mess."

"I don't think anyone wants to hurt me. What would be the point?"

"Whoever did this might think you know more than you really do."

That hadn't occurred to me. The idea made goose bumps rise on my arm.

The next morning, I ran into Leigh Dafoe at the elevator bank. Dafoe was a native San Franciscan from a prominent family. She had glossy dark hair, keen patrician features, and a little body with even smaller bones. She looked me over from head to toe and said, with the same fear and suspicion that always radiated from her eyes in the presence of African-Americans, "We need to talk right away."

"We need to talk right away" suggested that I was not going to start my day by meeting with our art director to continue an ongoing battle over a minstrel-show-type cover illustration which I refused to approve. It implied that a conference call I had arranged for nine-thirty was going to fall through. It hinted that I was about to be fired by the second-in-command for running away from our leader when she needed me to protect her from a grisly death.

I was trembling with fear as we were swept along with a horde of others into the elevator. When we stepped off the elevator at the sixth floor, I said, "Let me hang up my coat and then . . ."

"No. Now."

It was like a death march. Staffers murmured "Good morning," unable to resist staring at me as I moved swiftly behind Leigh through the corridors. Leigh unlocked her office door, slammed it behind me, and flicked on the lights. Without bothering to put down her briefcase, she came straight to the point.

"Craig Murray called me last night. He needs to know . . . I need to know . . . Sarah Jane needs to know . . . indeed, every employee at Welburn Books needs to know what you were doing at Annabelle's place on the morning she was murdered."

I didn't want to answer Leigh Dafoe's questions, but I was afraid of getting fired.

"I stopped by to pick up my appointment book. Who is Sarah Jane?"

"She is Annabelle's sister. Are you saying that Annabelle was in possession of your book?"

"Yes."

"How did she get it?"

"I left it at her house by accident two days before."

"What were you doing at her house two days before?"

I wanted to tell Leigh about the Moms Mabley manuscript but Craig now owned the company and I was afraid to anger him by revealing his secret.

"You'll have to ask Craig about that."

The Thin Pink Line formed instantly.

"I'm asking *you!* "

"Well, I'm sorry, Leigh, but I just can't tell you."

"Why not?"

"I was sworn to secrecy by Annabelle. She didn't want

you or anyone else to know about the project I was working on."

Silence.

"This is a real mess."

I agreed. "Yes, it is."

Silence.

All of a sudden, I knew that Leigh hadn't called me in to fire me. She simply wanted information.

"Why would a hotshot attorney like Keith Williams get involved in something so trivial as a lost appointment book?"

I didn't answer.

"Craig Murray wants to talk to you."

"He has my home number."

"What?" It came out as a gasp.

I stepped forward. "Where is Craig?"

She backed up until her desk was between us. "He is on the way over. The three of us will meet in the conference room and get to the bottom of this."

I shook my head. "Not without Keith."

"Well, then I suggest you get him over here, because your job is on the line."

Leigh's words, tone, and body language were brave, tough, unyielding—but, as usual, I could smell her fear and it made me angry. Why was she so scared? What did she see when she looked at me? A big, black, vicious grizzly bear with braided fur instead of a stocky, brown-skinned, ink-stained editorial drone?

"Fine, I'll do just that."

Down Editors' Row I marched, passing the open doors of my brethren who were already caught up in the ceaseless mini-dramas that were part and parcel of American book publishing.

". . . she wants a six figure advance for that piece of crap . . ."

". . . you promised me a first look at his next work . . ."

". . . it's a Black book. I'll have to run it by Jacqueline Blue before I can give you an answer . . ."

". . . I figured out who the killer was in the first chapter . . ."

". . . Oprah doesn't pick funny books. It needs a dysfunctional family in it, for chrissakes . . ."

". . . the book is in production now—you can't change the ending . . ."

". . . Governor Cuomo will sue our asses off if we print this . . ."

There was only one male voice in the chorus. Our industry, which 100 years ago had been a club for white, privileged, Ivy League males, was now a ladies' room crammed primarily with their latter-day counterparts— upper middle class, white, female, trust-fund babies. Of course, each one of the giant publishing houses (with one glaring, stubborn exception) had an African-American editor on staff, but the Thin Pink Lines kept us in such deep check that we never produced anything really innovative or revolutionary for Black book buyers. In spite of all this, I'd been in love with books all my life, and assisting in their creation was the only type of work I wanted to do.

Your job is on the line. A loud, rumbling noise filled my head and I breathed deeply—in and out, in and out— to quiet it as I approached Asha's desk. She was on the phone, giggling during what was obviously a personal call, and held her hand up in a *wait* motion when she saw me. Held her hand up! No doubt my previously hardworking assistant had seen my end run across Annabelle's lobby on the news last night and reached the conclusion that my days at Welburn Books were numbered.

"Get off the phone," I commanded.

"Girl, I'll call you back," she whispered into the receiver.

"What was that?" I did the *wait* sign.

"I'm sorry." Her voice was contrite. Her expression did not match.

I ignored the half-assed apology. "Get me Keith Williams and then Paul Dodson. When I'm done with them, bring in your project status report so I can make a list of what needs to be accomplished this week." I turned to leave but the loud, rumbling noise in my head had returned. "Asha, look at me."

She looked up.

"Do you like your job?"

Asha fumbled for words. "Yes . . . I . . . of course . . . I'm sorry."

"Then don't ever disrespect me like that again."

She tried to say something else but I gave her a *stop* signal and retreated to my office.

Both Keith and Paul were in meetings, and I was too shaken and out of control to debate the minstrel cover without losing my temper or participate in the conference call, so I closed the door and tidied up my work space.

By noon, I had rearranged my 100-plus books. They were now lined up neatly in alphabetical order on two white pine bookshelves. It was time to clean the mess that was my desk. I had removed the stapler, paper clip holder, and Scotch tape dispenser before realizing that some sort of weird dust had come off on my hands.

15

TAPPED?

The police had obviously dusted my office for finger-prints. Again, I lifted the receiver. Paul was still in a meeting. Keith was on his other line. I told his secretary that I would hold until he was free no matter how long it took.

I rocked back and forth in my ergonomically correct executive chair with my eyes closed, imagining Detective Marcus Gilchrist poking his sausage-like fingers around in the papers on my desk.

Had the computer department given the police my access code so they could read my e-mail? I chuckled at the thought. There were no homicidal thoughts in my computer files. Only endless e-mails to Victor Bell, over the past year, much of which had gone unanswered.

Given all the ruckus going on about Annabelle's death, Victor would probably come to Black Pack next Friday. Why did I still want Victor after the vulgar e-mail he'd sent me? A therapist would say I was suffering from low self-esteem, but who knows? Maybe he and I are soul mates and we'll just have to work all this out in another life.

I had just started mentally searching my wardrobe for an outfit he hadn't seen when Keith Williams barked into the phone.

"What's the problem, Jackie?"

He sounded annoyed and I was about to reprimand him for his abrupt manner when I remembered that I couldn't afford his services and how lucky I was to have him on the line. I told him about my conversation with Leigh Dafoe and the powder in my office which I thought was fingerprint dust.

"Jackie, I want you to calm down. The police are just doing their job. They have to try and match all the prints inside the house to people that the victim knew. Anyway, they expect to find your prints—we've admitted that you were there twice in forty-eight hours. So, what is the problem?"

I felt slightly ridiculous but there was one point left. "Craig is down the hall in Leigh Dafoe's office. She hinted this morning that if I don't talk to them, I'll lose my job. Can you come over here?"

"Okay, I'll be there as soon as I can. What I need you to do in the meantime is relax and go about your business as normally as possible. That means you should buy and sell books, talk to your colleagues about anything except this case, and try not to look anxious. Okay?"

"That detective may have put all kinds of strange thoughts in Craig's head. What if he says something terrible like 'Jackie, why did you kill my wife?' "

Keith's voice turned hard. "Did you hear what you just said on a company phone that may be tapped? Just for the record, did you kill Craig Murray's wife?"

"No, I did not."

"Then I suggest that you hunker down and do what Welburn Books is paying you to do."

I felt utterly stupid. "I'm sorry."

"No problem. I'll see you in about half an hour."

There was a click and Keith Williams was gone.

Even though I was a nervous wreck, I still needed to settle the cover feud. Normally, editors do not have any control over what their author's cover will look like, but due to Annabelle's insistence, Helen, the art director, had to get my approval on the covers that were aimed at African-American readers. When I saw the direction that the artists were taking for Willow Van Silver's latest romance novel, I hit the roof. It was one of those cartoony-looking covers with the usual screaming primary colors.

I took the cover with me down to Helen's office and knocked on her door. She looked up and gave me a faint smile which turned to a Thin Pink Line when she caught sight of the sketch in my hand.

"Good morning, Jackie."

"Hello," I answered pleasantly. "May I sit down?"

She nodded at the empty guest chair and I sat.

"Is there a problem, Jackie?"

Helen knew goddamned well there was a problem. She'd had her assistant deliver the cover to my office and I had refused to sign off on it.

"Actually, there is. Perhaps we can work out a solution together."

She didn't want me to take this conciliatory approach. What she wanted was for me to flat-out accuse her of not understanding the audience that the cover was meant to reach so that she could go screaming to Leigh that I was "too sensitive" about racial issues. We'd been down this road many times and I had no intention of falling into that trap today.

"What do you think the cover needs?" she inquired through gritted teeth.

"Well," I answered pleasantly, "perhaps you could tone down this screaming red, put some faces on the characters instead of blanking them out . . . better yet, you could hire real people to pose for it."

"Anything else?" she snapped.

"Yes. Do you think it is appropriate that both the man and woman are doing a jitterbug with their butts arched high in the air? I mean, the book is about a teacher and the handsome pediatrician who has come into her life. They aren't dancers."

Helen leaned back and folded her arms across her chest. "Why must you and I go through this with just about every cover that is created for your books?"

This was my cue to say something that she could twist around to make me sound like an unreasonable militant.

I stood up and gazed at her with a sympathetic expression on my face. "Why, Helen, I didn't realize you felt that way. Let's go to lunch real soon and I'll be happy to listen to all your concerns and ideas. All right?"

She just stared at me—all angry eyes and red cheeks set above the Thin Pink Line—and said nothing.

I slammed her door on my way out.

16

REPRIEVE

There was a flurry of excitement in the hallways when Keith arrived. People stared, waved, smiled, and more than a few women preened in his direction. I led him into Leigh's office.

Craig greeted me like a long-lost friend. He seemed to have aged in the last two weeks. He stood up like a gentleman, shook Keith's hand, gave me a chest-crushing hug, and kissed me on the cheek when I entered Leigh's office, but he didn't smile. His eyebrows were furrowed in concentration and there were worry lines that I didn't remember seeing before across his forehead. His eyes were those of a sad child. I murmured my condolences into his ear, gave him a comforting pat on the back, and sat down in the second guest chair, which meant that we were all facing Leigh, and I had to twist slightly whenever I wanted to address Craig directly.

"Craig, I tried to reach you several times during that awful first week, but you were either out or not taking calls."

He gave me a tired smile. "Thanks, Jackie. I'm really happy to see you."

"How is Dora?"

He leaned back and sighed. "Ahh, Pixie. She is absolutely destroyed . . . just destroyed . . . I'm looking for a good child psychiatrist to help her through all this. It would help a lot if the police could find this dirtbag and we could all get some kind of closure."

Leigh was watching us closely. Like all the editors, I reported directly to Leigh, and she had reported to Annabelle. She was wondering how I got so close to the chief and her husband.

I understood how she felt. If Asha and Leigh started hanging out, I would feel annoyed and disrespected also. But it wasn't my fault and it was time she knew the truth.

"Craig, I didn't tell Leigh about the Mabley book because Annabelle asked me not to, but Leigh is my supervisor and all this secrecy is beginning to cause problems between us."

He seemed befuddled. "Problems?"

Leigh placed her hands flat on the desk. "If Jackie has a good reason for that dash across your lobby on the morning of Annabelle's death, then we need to hear it. Otherwise, it will be impossible for her to work here with a terrible cloud of suspicion hanging over her head."

Keith interrupted. "Ms. Blue cannot be fired. She has not even been charged, let alone convicted of any crime."

Leigh turned red.

"I don't know why Jackie came to see Annabelle that morning but I assume it was to apologize to Annabelle," Craig said.

What the hell was he talking about?

"Apologize?" I asked.

"Annabelle said you were so angry when she told you that the promotion was going to someone else that you left without saying good-bye to her. When I saw the newscast, I figured you apologized for your behavior and ran across the lobby because you were late for work."

I said nothing.

"I guess I was wrong," he continued. "So, why were you there?"

I told him about the lost Filofax.

He shrugged. "Yeah, I do remember you writing in that book when we met in the library."

Leigh could take no more. "Met in the library? What was the meeting about?"

Craig stood up. "Call an emergency meeting, Leigh. I want all employees gathered together so I only have to tell the story once. Welburn Books needs Jackie and they need to understand that if there is any intrigue afoot here, it was the one my wife and I created."

He was the new boss. Leigh did as she was told. I felt lighter than I had since my nerve-rattling meeting with Detective Gilchrist.

This time, all 300 employees were packed in the conference room; at Craig's insistence, I was standing in the front between Craig and Leigh. To say I felt uncomfortable at being put on the spot would be a gigantic understatement.

"I'm Craig Murray and it is good to meet all of you. I had planned to meet with you soon and have a discussion about my vision and plans for Welburn Books over the next few years. However, I understand that last night's newscast, with its emphasis on Jacqueline Blue, has left you all very concerned. I'm here now to clear up any rumors, dark thoughts, or misconceptions about her that you may have."

He told the story of his fascination with Moms Mabley and how it was Annabelle's idea that I help him on the project. "Jackie worked very hard on her days off with no extra compensation to shape this biography into the work of art that it is now."

Work of art? It was a piece of shit!

"My wife felt that it would smack of nepotism if she published *All About Moms* here at Welburn, but now I think this is the best place for it. Why should another house and some other editor get the credit after Jackie worked so hard? So, when this terrible business is over, we'll get to work, put it on the schedule, and place Miss Mabley's story in the hands of readers everywhere. I'll let Jackie tell you about her mad dash across my lobby which the media has managed to turn into something sinister."

For what seemed like the hundredth time, I told the story of meeting Craig to work on *All About Moms,* accidentally leaving my portable organizing system in the Murray home, and racing to meet Jamal Hunt. "As you know," I concluded, "Jamal is the newest and brightest star on the Welburn roster."

I walked Keith out to the elevator. "What do you think?" I asked anxiously.

He whispered into my ear. "Up until this morning, Craig Murray was at the top of my list. But that man did not kill his wife and now I have no idea who did."

17

BACK AT THE PACK

I got the clear sensation that I was the subject of mucho gossip when I reached the Black Pack table the next Friday night. Who could blame them?

They were all in attendance and the waiter had pushed three tables together to accommodate the group. My eyes locked with Victor's as I stood beside an empty chair, and for a moment I didn't hear or see anything else in the room. Not the cluster of thirsty people crowded around the bar, the framed photographs of the restaurant's celebrity owner, not even Paul, who was saying something to me as he tugged at my sleeve. My heart was hammering—I forgot all about Victor's humiliating e-mail. I just wanted to throw myself at his feet and worship him like an Egyptian god.

His skin was the color of deep, dark Godiva chocolate; he had close-cropped black hair with a razor part on the right side, thick, dark lips, and big, sexy eyes which rivaled those of the long-dead movie star, Bette Davis.

I might have stood there frozen forever if Paul had not sucked his teeth so loudly that the people at the next table turned around and stared. It broke me out of my trance and I hastily sat down.

My African-American sisters and brothers welcomed me like I was an escaped slave who had managed to get to their collective hiding place somewhere in Canada. It felt warm and sweet enough to make me burst into tears, but that would have made my well-applied makeup run down my cheeks, and I was not about to let that happen in front of Victor. So, I blinked hard a few times and stared at Rachel's blond pouf of hair, which formed a halo around her blue-black skin, until I felt a giggle coming up in my throat.

"Okay, what were y'all saying about me before I came in," I said, to lighten the moment.

"Paul was telling us how he hooked you up with Keith Williams. Girl, it would be worth doing twenty years in jail if you could end up with him afterward," Rachel laughed.

"I'm not interested in Keith."

All I want is Victor Bell is what I started to say, but that would have been way over the top.

"Did Keith buy you that hot pink suit?" Rachel continued. "It is to die for."

I fingered the gold buttons on my new suit, which was actually a deep, flattering fuchsia. "Of course not."

"You should have worn that suit when you did your end run across that lobby, girlfriend. Because that coat you had on was not working. It made you look like two tons of fun." This was from Dallas, but there was relief in her eyes and I knew she was really glad to see me.

Everyone laughed.

"Well," I replied while picking up the menu which I knew by heart, "I'll make sure that I'm wearing Versace the next time murder comes a-callin'."

Once I used the word "murder," they felt free to pelt me with questions.

"Do the police have any suspects?"

"Is Keith Williams as fine in person as he looks on TV?"

"Paul said you were there to get your Filofax. What was it doing there?"

"Do you know who the killer is?"

Paul tapped a fork on the side of his water glass. "Hold up, everybody—Jackie can't talk about the case until the police have solved it."

"That's cool." Victor had a voice like warm chocolate syrup dripping over a hot peach cobbler. "I'm just glad that Jackie is all right."

I practically swooned. Maybe he would quit his girlfriend, whoever she was, and rescue a damsel-in-distress like me.

During the hubbub of ordering meals and drinks, I managed to sneak a few sidelong glances at the object of my desire. Each time, he was either engaged in heated conversation with Joe Long, who was seated on his right, or staring in concentration at the wine list.

"Why don't you just go and sit in his lap?" Paul whispered nastily.

"What is the matter with you?" I asked innocently.

I knew perfectly well what the matter was.

"Nothing," he answered brusquely.

I decided not to look at Victor for the rest of the meal so that Paul could relax and enjoy himself.

"So, Victor, tell us what the bookstore owners are asking for these days," Elaine "I went to Harvard" Garner said as she actually took out a pad and pen to record his answers.

Victor Bell was the only one in the group who didn't have to deal with office politics. He was a sales rep and his job was to go from bookstore to bookstore in the territory assigned to him and convince them to order large quantities of whatever books his company was publishing.

Alyssa rushed in just then, and there was a lot of air-kissing and moving chairs around to make room for her before Victor could tell his story.

Looking extremely self-conscious at being the center of attention, Victor Bell declared that he had just returned from a three-day trip down the East Coast. Without telling us the names of the stores or their buyers, he related stories of coming across many people who made crucial decisions even though they had not heard of many Black celebrities who had books in the upcoming catalog.

"Do you believe that these white buyers had never heard of Steve Harvey?"

There were cries of "oh, come on" and "you gotta be kiddin'."

"I'm serious as sickle cell, y'all. I had to explain who he was over and over again. In the end, one of the stores took five and the others would only order two."

"This is so disheartening," said Elaine. "We work our butts off and run into one wall after another. But you didn't answer my question. What is it that they're looking for?"

Victor sighed. "Another *Waiting to Exhale*. If I were you guys, I'd buy as much fiction I could. They can't get enough of it."

"Some of the large bookstore chains are even worse," Victor continued after downing half a glass of straight Scotch. "They have a different buyer for each category."

"Each category?" asked Dallas.

"Yes. They have a mystery buyer, a health book buyer, a fiction buyer, and on and on. Every single one of them is white. To tell you the truth, I like the days when I hit the road with the mainstream catalog. I hate meeting with these people about the Black books. It is a constant process of education, education, and education. It is way too exhausting."

"What I wanna know is who this asshole thought Steve Harvey was when you first mentioned his name," said Paul.

We hung onto every word that Victor had to say. "I only had two minutes to make my pitch. I told him that I had Steve Harvey's biography coming up. The guy looks at me and says, "Who is that?" I said, 'Come on, man, you gotta know who Steve Harvey is.' The man has his own TV show and he sold out Madison Square Garden for his standup comedy act without even advertising. The guy listens and then says, 'oh that guy! I'm glad to hear he is workin' again because he was real sick and in a wheelchair, last I heard.' Well, at first I didn't know what he was talking about. But after a while, I realized he was talkin' 'bout Richard Pryor."

We all laughed to keep from crying.

18

PURE BLISS

So, Paul and I joked over the awkwardness between us, and the office hummed along in its usual pattern. Pam Silberstein and I started having lunch together again.

Mama and Elvira went on a bus ride to Atlantic City around Valentine's Day and Mama won $200. They also decided to join a church, even though Mama hadn't set foot in one since her best friend betrayed her.

In short, for three weeks my life drifted back into some semblance of normalcy.

One evening, I had my coat on and a shopping bag of manuscripts in hand when Asha buzzed me on the intercom. I hesitated—the last thing I needed was to get stuck in a lengthy conversation. She buzzed again and I answered.

"Yes, Asha?"

"Victor Bell is on line one. Will you take it?"

Will rain stay wet?

"Sure."

"Hello, Victor . . . how are you?"

"I'm fine, dear, and you?"

Dear? He had come to his senses and was ready to snuggle me securely close to his massive chest. Surely heaven couldn't be any better than this. I'd have to go on a diet, get my hair rebraided, get some black silk sheets for my queen-sized bed. Actually, maybe I'd better invest in a king-sized bed since Victor was so tall. My apartment needed a fresh paint job and new window coverings. Maybe Levelor vertical blinds . . . gold for the living room and a nice blush for the bedroom . . .

"Jackie, are you there?"

Good Lord, the man had been talking while my mind wandered. "Yes, I'm here. What were you saying?"

"I asked if you were free to have dinner with me tonight."

"What about your girlfriend?" It just popped out of my mouth. He probably had some business problem he wanted to talk with me about and now I had shown my desperation yet again. I immediately wished that a rope would magically appear on my desk so I could coil one end of it around my throat and the other over something heavy enough to help me end my stupid-ass life.

"We're not together anymore. Forget about it."

"That was a very nasty message, Victor. It really hurt my feelings."

"I'm sorry. Something pretty bad happened to me that day and I took it out on you. Will you let me treat you to some food and drink?"

I was so happy, it was hard not to pump my fist in the air and cheer. I really wanted to go out with him but not in the outfit I was wearing—a starched white blouse with ruffles at the neck and wrists, which made me look like Prince, and a plain, ankle-length black skirt. "Can I take a raincheck?"

"Sure. What about tomorrow?" He sounded desperate.

What the hell was going on?

"Yes."

"Good. I'll pick you up at your office around five-thirty. Is that all right?"

"It is."

All the way home, I wished there was someone I could talk to about Victor's strange and sudden change of heart. Mama would be so angry to know that I'd been chasing a man who didn't want me for the past year that asking her advice was absolutely unthinkable.

Paul was out of the question. Victor was the one sore subject between us. He was also spending less time at my house since he started seeing Rosa with the crooked nose. On the one hand, I felt sorry for her because Paul was only using her to make me jealous, and on the other, knowing that with one crook of my little finger she would be manless gave me an odd feeling of power.

Pam Silberstein stopped by my office the next day at noon. "Wow! Are we eating at The Four Seasons today?"

I was wearing a black, knee-length dress with suede curlicues around the heart-shaped neckline, a diamond teardrop pendant with matching earrings, and my long braids were curled and pinned into a stylish French roll.

I pulled my purse out of a desk drawer and grinned. "This isn't about you. I have a date tonight."

"You look marvelous. He won't be able to take his eyes off of you."

As I put my coat on and followed Pam toward the elevators, I hoped that she was right.

Pam waited until we were seated at Café Un Deux Trois on 44th Street and had ordered our food—salmon with béarnaise sauce for me, French onion soup and a Caesar salad for her—before she hit me with the news.

"I'm leaving Welburn, Jackie. I gave Leigh my resignation this morning."

"Do you have another job?"

She smiled triumphantly. "You're looking at the new head of trade paperbacks for Hamilton Welsh & Hamilton."

I was sad for me and happy for her. "Oh, Pam. It won't be the same without you."

"I'm going to miss you, too, kid. There is another opening at Hamilton for a senior editor and I wish you would consider taking it."

Oh, what a tempting offer! To get away from Craig's offensive book, Annabelle's dark, empty office, the atmosphere of grim uncertainty. It would be so easy to pack up and walk away from it all but then I would look as though I had something to hide.

I shook my head. "The media is still harping on the morning I was rushing to meet with Jamal. As soon as Annabelle's killer is behind bars, I'll be glad to leave Welburn Books. If I make a move before that, it will look very bad for me."

She toyed with her silverware. "Have you heard anything more about the investigation?"

"Only what I read in the papers."

And then I remembered Alyssa. "Pam, I know an extremely talented editor who is looking for a new senior editor spot. Would you take a look at her resumé?"

"Absolutely. Did she get laid off or something?"

I started telling her Alyssa's story and her face got redder and redder as I went on.

"That's horrible," Pam said when I finished. "You tell Alyssa that I'd like to see her right away. I'm going to make sure she gets a job and if Marlene Rashker doesn't like it, I don't give a damn."

"Thanks, Pam." I felt pleased.

Our food arrived and we dug in with gusto.

"Tell me something, Jackie. Is Craig Murray's book any good?"

"Just between you and me?"

"I swear." She crossed her heart.

"It's pure crap."

She burst out laughing and coughing into her napkin. "I knew it. You poor dear. Can it be fixed?"

"Hell, no."

"Did you tell Annabelle?"

"I let her know that it had a ridiculous premise, but of course I said I could fix it. She really didn't want to hear anything else."

Pam shook her head and took a sip of water. "That's why I'm getting out. Craig Murray seems like a nice guy but he's going to run the company into the ground and take a whole lot of reputations with him. Mine won't be one of them."

"Craig is a very nice man," I agreed.

"I don't think he killed her," Pam said quietly.

Keith had said the same thing but I pretended the thought had never occurred to me. "Craig? A killer? Why would you say something like that?"

"Oh, come on, Jackie. He is probably suspect number one on the police blotter. The husband always is. He stands to inherit a great deal of money."

I swallowed a piece of salmon. "True, but I've been watching *Columbo* for years and there must be motive, means, and opportunity. Craig didn't have the opportunity. Keith has learned that he and Dora spent the night at his sister's house. He took Dora to preschool on the morning of the murder and when I stopped by, he still had not come home."

Pam drummed her fingers on the table. "I watch *Columbo*, too, and there was this one case where the husband left a building and then went around to a back alley and shimmied up a drainpipe to get back in the house. He murdered his wife and then went back down the pipe to a local bar where dozens of people could see him and furnish an alibi."

"Pam, I doubt that there is an alley or drainpipe in the back of The Dakota."

She was really into it now. "Don't be so sure that Craig couldn't reenter the building unseen. Suppose he bribed a maintenance worker to open a side door or something?"

"Then he'd have to kill the maintenance worker or he'd always have to worry about the guy double-crossing him."

Pam thought that over for a moment. "Maybe the worker was in the country illegally. He could be back in Santo Domingo or wherever by now."

Her theory made sense but I didn't want the game to stop. "Let's forget Craig for a minute. How about an angry neighbor? After I leave, he slips up to Annabelle's place, does the dirty deed, and takes the elevator back up or down to his own apartment. That's why he isn't seen on the lobby videotape. The sister goes up, finds the body, and runs screaming down to the lobby."

"How did the sister get into the apartment?"

I shrugged. "She must have a key."

"Okay, what is the neighbor so angry about?"

"Maybe he wrote a book, Annabelle read it, and refused to publish it."

This sent Pam into gales of laughter. "Isn't it awful when you let people know that you work in publishing? I've had pages thrust at me by my lawyer, dry cleaner, and even the woman who does my nails."

"I stopped telling folks what I do for a living a long time ago."

We talked shop after that for a while and then paid the check. On the way back to the office, I made a mental note to put Alyssa and Pam together.

The rest of my day was spent in splendid anticipation.

Victor had chosen a fine, upscale Chinese restaurant

called *A Dish of Salt,* which was a few blocks away, and as we walked along chatting pleasantly, I marveled at how quickly my dreary existence had been transformed. After weeks of dread, sadness, and panic, I was now moving closer to my dream of true love in the arms of Victor Bell.

"Where do you live?" I asked curiously.

"In Park Slope. I'm a native Brooklynite."

He went on to tell me that he was an only child, raised by a single parent. His mother was a nurse who now lived in San Francisco with her second husband in a house that was much too big for the two of them. "It's psychological," he said. "We always lived in such small apartments that now she's gone overboard."

Well! Paul and I had built our friendship on the fact that we were the only two members of the Black Pack who did not come from upper middle-class homes. All the rest of them were the children of professional parents who attended private schools, were able to afford music and dance lessons, braces for unruly teeth, and household help for cooking and cleaning. Paul's youth had been even more deprived than mine. We always listened in jealous amazement at Black Pack meetings when some of the others talked about their young lives, which seemed straight out of the Cosby show.

Now, it seemed that Victor might have more in common with Paul and me than he did with the others.

"Money was tight in my house, too." I offered him the opening shyly.

He looked down at me in surprise. "Mom and I didn't have financial problems. Registered nurses do pretty well, you know. My problem was loneliness. She had to work the night shift a lot and I didn't have anyone to play with."

Allrighty then, I'd have to find some other way to bond with him.

I chuckled lightly. "I'm an only child, too. When I get

married, I'm going to have a houseful of kids so they'll have plenty of playmates."

He looked uncomfortable and that's when I remembered that you were never supposed to mention the word "marriage" on a first date.

"So how is work coming along?" I asked hastily.

"Not as well as I'd like. I was up for district manager a few weeks ago and the job went to someone else."

By now we'd reached the restaurant and we waited for a few minutes until a table became available. I was still full from the salmon I'd had at lunch. What could I order that was light and yet plentiful enough to keep Victor at the table for a long time?

When we were seated, he gave me a sexy smile. "Thanks for coming out with me."

He should thank me five hundred times. After referring to my vagina as a THAT! Maybe I should give it a name . . . something elegant like Grace, in case another man did the same thing to me. I would haughtily reply, *Her name is not THAT. It is Grace.*

Victor was looking at me curiously. "A penny for your thoughts."

"I was thinking about what you said about the district manager position," I lied smoothly. "The same thing happened to me recently."

He sighed and spread his napkin over his lap. "I'm going to open my own business. I'm sick of this kind of nonsense. These decisions are not based on ability . . . it's all politics."

We ordered wonton soup and agreed to share some kind of shrimp dish. He asked the waiter to bring him a straight vodka on the rocks.

"Why don't you want a drink?"

Because I'll end up telling you about the pornographic dreams I have about you at least three times a week, I thought.

"I've just started a new diet."

"You look fine to me just the way you are."

The gods were smiling down on me.

"Thanks."

"So, tell me about the job you didn't get."

"It's the next step up the editorial ladder. I've done mysteries, romance, suspense, biography, every category I could think of over the past five years so that I'd be ready for an executive editor slot if one opened up. Well, one did open up and my boss gave it to a woman named Astrid Norstromm."

"Did she give you a reason?"

"She said that Astrid had worked in a wider variety of categories. What she really meant was that all my work was with Black authors. Astrid's authors are all white."

"Damn! What did you say to her?"

"Nothing. Not a word. I got up and walked out."

"Was that before or after the CEO was killed?"

"My conversation was with the CEO. She got killed the next day."

Victor was about to say something when a thought suddenly occurred to me.

"Wait a minute! Annabelle never had the chance to announce her decision. I wonder . . ."

"You wonder if it's too late," Victor observed quietly. "It is too late. By the time Annabelle talked with you, the paperwork on this other woman was already done and processed. That is how the corporate machine works. They're just waiting until a decent amount of time has passed before they start announcing promotions and such. After all, the poor woman's killer is still on the loose."

He was right.

"Oh, well," I offered lamely. "Better luck next time."

He hunched forward and stared at me intently. "Tell me, Jackie. Did you see anyone lurking around the building that morning?"

"What building?"

"When you ran out of the lobby . . . did you see anyone you knew?"

What an odd question for Victor to ask. "No. I was too intent on getting a cab. Was there someone around who I should have noticed?"

"I'm . . . well, um . . . of course not."

I finished the last drop of my soup and let the spoon clatter into the bowl. "That reminds me—I saw you at Annabelle's funeral. What were you doing there?"

"We met once years ago at an industry function," he replied smoothly. "I was just getting started as a sales rep in publishing. She was nice enough to answer all my stupid questions. I figured the least I could do was show up and pay my respects."

"The whole thing is just so sad."

He leaned back in his chair and sighed. "Yeah. Are the police close to making an arrest?"

I shrugged. "Maybe Keith knows, but no one has told me a thing."

He took a sip of vodka. "This murder has got everyone in the city all cranked up."

We moved on to other topics and soon I was wondering more about how to get invited into his Park Slope bedroom than anything else.

19

MISS NIXON

Victor made no move to seduce me the night before. Like a perfect gentleman, he thanked me for a pleasant evening and put my horny behind in a cab. I spent my night dreaming of the two of us locked in a series of feverish, fantasy sexual positions. When the phone rang, I groaned and willed it to go away. I wasn't ready to let Victor go just yet. It stopped and started ringing again insistently.

"Hello."

"Jackie, it's Paul. Wake up, girl, all hell is about to break loose."

"What time is it?"

"It's eight. Get up, throw something on, go out and buy the *Comet*. Then call me back."

I swung my feet onto the floor. "Is it about Annabelle's murder?"

"Stop talking and get the paper, Jackie."

Paul hung up.

I threw my coat on over my nightgown, slipped my feet into a pair of loafers, and hit the street with my sleep-encrusted eyes and unwashed body, looking like a madwoman.

The chilly, winter-morning air had pierced through my coat, danced under my flannel pajamas, and wrapped itself around my naked skin by the time I turned onto 111th Street where the little Spanish man stood hawking his newspapers. I dug two quarters out of my coat pocket, pressed them into his hand, and raced back home, hugging the *New York Comet* to my chest.

I sat down on the sofa without removing my coat and started to read. The headline blared *FORMER DEBU-TANTE'S MURDER STILL UNSOLVED*. The front page was divided lengthwise by a thick, black line. On the left side was a photo of Annabelle, looking young and fresh in a floor-length white gown. A white corsage was pinned to her wrist. The caption underneath it said: Eighteen-year-old Annabelle Welburn, on the eve of her society debut. The right photo showed Annabelle on the beach, throwing a ball at a tiny, dark-haired tot who was clapping her hands in glee. The caption underneath that one said: Annabelle Welburn Murray and her two-year-old daughter, Dora. The pictures were touching but no reason for Paul to wake me up at eight in the morning.

There were more pictures of Annabelle with various family members inside and two lengthy stories about Annabelle's life as a prep school student and her years at Vassar. I was about to close the paper and call Paul when the name "Gilchrist" in Tiffany Nixon's column caught my eye. It read:

WRAPPED IN A PC CLOAK
by Tiffany Nixon

> *So Detective Marcus Gilchrist has a videotape of some-one with a grudge against poor Annabelle Welburn Murray running away from the scene of her murder. The*

district attorney knows where the woman lives and works and yet neither man is making any moves toward an arrest in this month-old case. Why not? Because the woman on the tape is wrapped in a cloak called Political Correctness.

The press also seems willing to let the videotape slide under the rug, accepting a celebrity attorney's word that the woman's sprint was toward a business appointment rather than away from a body with its throat twisted and mangled like an obscene, oversized doll. Why? Because the woman on the tape is Black from a humble background and the victim is white and rich.

Fear of political incorrectness has turned the media away from the obvious and paralyzed the New York City Police Department.

The ridiculous PC awareness which runs rampant through our society has long been the bread and butter of standup comics, but it isn't funny. In this case it is downright appalling.

I was perched on the edge of my sofa in a semi-trance, struggling to determine which was more horrific: the fact that the writer of such racist trash was a Black woman, or her thinly veiled allegation that I was a cold-blooded killer who was being spared the electric chair simply because of my ethnicity.

The telephone chimed. It was Paul again.

"Jackie, did you read it?" he asked.

"I'm stunned."

"Honey, what grudge did you have against her?"

"I guess it means I was mad about the promotion." My heart was thumping against the wall of my chest with such force that I thought it was going to pop right out and fall to the floor at my feet. "I've got to get off the phone and try to reach Keith Williams."

"Call me back and let me know what he says. I won't leave for work until I hear back from you, okay?"

My heart thumped with anger and terror. "No. I'll get back to you when I can."

The only people I trusted at that moment were Mama and Keith. I wasn't worried that Mama would see the column because she only bought the *New York Daily News*. I concentrated on finding Keith. His secretary said he wasn't expected in until ten A.M. I couldn't bear to just sit in the apartment, and my instincts told me I needed legal advice before going anywhere near the offices of Welburn Books. So I decided to cool my heels in the waiting room at Keith's law firm.

Finding a yellow cab on my street was nearly impossible, even though plenty of whites had moved into Harlem. So, I took a Gypsy cab down to Trump Tower and the driver charged me twenty dollars, which pissed me off even more. A young man was sitting at the reception desk.

"Hi, my name is Jacqueline Blue. I know Keith isn't in yet but I'd like to just sit here and wait for him if you don't mind."

"Is he expecting you?" The young man had close-cropped brown hair and the beginnings of a moustache.

I was in no mood for protocol. "If he has read the *New York Comet* this morning, he is certainly expecting at least a phone call from me. Now please, may I just sit down?"

"Mr. Williams is in his office," the young man said smoothly. "I'll let him know you're here."

The pint-sized secretary was wearing another expensive suit and I wondered how much Keith paid his staff. She beckoned me to follow her and I did.

There was no music coming out of the sound system and Keith was on the phone.

I sat down in the same guest chair facing Keith that I had used on my first visit.

Keith ended his call and came all the way around the desk to shake my hand before sitting down again.

"Did you see that column in the paper this morning?" I cried out anxiously.

"I did."

"Well, what should I do?"

Keith was noticeably uneasy. "You have got big problems, Jackie." He sighed and repeated himself, "Big problems."

He said "you," not "we"! My God, he was pulling out!

I was desperate. "Listen, Keith, I know I can't afford you but if you'll just help me out a little longer, I promise I'll pay your bill even if I have to work two jobs when all this is over." My voice was rising to a shriek. "Please, you can't desert . . ."

He put a stop to my lament with the raise of his hand. "Calm down, Jackie. It's been almost three years since I took on a pro bono case. I'm not going anywhere because that would make you look guilty as hell and I don't believe you killed Annabelle Murray."

I actually wept with gratitude and he took a handkerchief from his breast pocket and gave it to me.

"Now, we've got a lot of work to do. Let's get to it. The police have ruled out burglary as a motive. There were several paintings on the premises valued at over three million dollars that weren't touched. The victim was still wearing an expensive pearl necklace and matching earrings when the body was found and her wallet, which was clearly visible, contained $500 in cash and several credit cards."

"So, the motive was personal," I replied.

"Yes."

"What on earth did Annabelle do to make someone so angry?"

"That's the $50,000 question, Jackie. Tell me, do you know a lot of journalists?"

"No. Most of my authors write fiction."

"Have you ever met the columnist Tiffany Nixon?"

"Yes."

"When, where, and why?"

"Last year at the office. She came in to meet with an editor named Astrid Norstromm about a book idea that she had. Since Tiffany Nixon is Black, I had to attend the meeting."

"Did the book get published?"

"Not by Welburn. It was a horrible idea . . . some right wing, conservative rant against Black colleges, affirmative action . . . I don't remember it all but it was truly nauseating."

"Did you tell her how you felt about it?"

"No. She was Astrid's guest and that would have been inappropriate."

"Then what happened?"

"We listened to Miss Nixon's spiel and then Astrid walked her out to the reception area. When Astrid came back, I told her I would not support the acquisition when it reached the editorial board."

"What happened at the board meeting?"

"Astrid didn't bring it up. I never heard about it again."

"Do you think Astrid told Miss Nixon that it was you who jettisoned her chances?"

"We're not supposed to let a prospective author know about stuff like that, but Astrid hates me, so she might have."

"I want to hear all about your problems with Astrid but not right now."

"Okay. I have to call my job and tell them I'm on my way. May I use your phone?"

"Jackie, someone in that office may be trying to set you up. I'll talk to whoever is in charge and arrange a paid leave-of-absence for you until this case is closed."

"My authors need me, Keith. Can't I just work from home?"

"Jackie, I was on the phone with a friend of mine when you came in. She is a high-ranking member of the police department and we've known each other a very long time. Your fingerprints have been found in the same bathroom where Mrs. Murray's body was found. By tomorrow morning, Tiffany Nixon will know that and the pressure on the police department to make an arrest will be tremendous. I sincerely doubt that the victim's family will allow you to take any company documents home to work on."

"So, if I had gone to work this morning . . ."

"They would have sent you home."

"Can they fire me just like that?"

"No, you haven't been indicted for the crime. However, under the circumstances they can suspend you until this serious matter has been cleared up. I'm going to try and arrange things so you will continue receiving a paycheck during that time. Understand?"

"Yes," I whispered.

"Now, can you explain how your fingerprints ended up at the murder scene?"

"I told you I was at the house two days before Annabelle died. I used that bathroom during the visit."

Keith ruffled through some papers and read two of them before addressing me again. "You told me that Annabelle let you in the apartment and you went down the hall by yourself to meet with her husband in the library."

"I stopped in the bathroom along the way."

Keith jumped up and slapped his desk with an open palm. The sound made me jump. He shoved the papers in my direction. "Find it!"

I threw my hands up helplessly. "Find what?"

"These are my notes from our first meeting and a

copy of the statement you gave to the police. I want you to find just one goddamned place in any of it where you say that you used the bathroom on that morning in the Murrays' apartment."

"It didn't seem important, so I guess I forgot to mention it." My voice was a whisper.

"You forgot to mention it. Even if Mrs. Murray saw you go into the bathroom, she isn't here to say so. Don't you know how convenient that piece of information is going to sound now?"

"I'm sorry."

"I'm going to call your employer now and when I'm done with that, you are going to tell me your life story. Do you hear me? Every single little thing you can remember doing, hearing, saying since the day you took your first breath. I'll tell you what to skip and when. Are we clear?"

"Yes."

He picked up the receiver and then paused. "Jackie, how much money do you have in the bank?"

I was confused. "About $10,000, I guess."

"That won't be enough."

"For what?"

"Bail, sweetheart," he replied angrily.

While Keith was on the phone wrangling with the Welburn lawyers, I reached the heartrending conclusion that by now everyone in the industry had seen Tiffany Nixon's article and my reputation was irreparably tarnished. With no job, hobbies, children, or significant other in my life, I would now have plenty of time to help with the investigation and thereby clear my name. When not running around the city playing amateur sleuth and visiting with Mama, would I have any viable friendships to keep my spirits up? Would Paul stand by me? Would Victor ask me out for another date? Would

Pam still help Alyssa get the job? What would the members of the Black Pack say?

I recalled my conversation with Alyssa two months before: *Well, don't worry about me, Alyssa. I am going to help you regardless of what anyone thinks.*

What about the rest of the Black Pack?

They're running so hard for cover, they might pass the ghost of Jesse Owens on the way.

If it had not been for me, the Black Pack would have kicked Alyssa to the curb and never mentioned her name again. I didn't really blame them then and I wasn't going to hold my banishment against them now. In fact, I felt badly about what they were going to have to suffer through in the coming weeks. In order to keep their jobs, they would have to repudiate me, denounce me, and hide any belief in my innocence in the presence of every single white person they encountered.

Dallas Mowrey was the type of Black who would wait until the subject arose before breaking into the old soft shoe. So would Joe Long.

Elaine and Rachel were the types who preferred to get their minstrel acts over with as quickly as possible. They would bring up the Jacqueline Blue matter first, practically disavow any knowledge of my birth, and endear themselves even more to their white coworkers and superiors.

Keith looked exhausted when he got off the phone. My salary and benefits would remain intact for the next eight weeks no matter what happened. After that, who knew?

20

MAMA

Keith didn't hear my whole life story but he came pretty damn close. I left out my obsession with Victor Bell. It was too embarrassing to discuss, and besides, I'd sound like some kind of nut case.

It was almost seven P.M. when I left his office, and except for a short break to scarf down a pizza that his secretary called out for, we had been talking about the publishing industry and the people who worked in it nonstop.

Keith was convinced that unless the real killer was apprehended almost immediately, the district attorney would respond to the intense media scrutiny by asking the grand jury to issue an indictment against me. He would not allow me to appear before a grand jury, and I had to prepare myself for a grim reality—the police would issue a warrant for my arrest. He told me that he had friends in high places so I'd be spared a humiliating perp walk in front of the television cameras and only spend a few hours in custody before bail was granted. Since I had a job, an elderly mother, and was a native

New Yorker, a case could be made that I was not a flight risk so I could get bail and remain free until my trial.

Arrested! My reputation would be ruined—I'd never get another job in my field and there was a good chance that Mama would be paralyzed by the shame. I nearly passed out in Keith's office. And how, pray tell, would I come up with bail money if the need should arise?

I dragged myself to Mama's house, wondering how I was going to tell her this terrible news.

When she opened the door to let me in, I was relieved to find Elvira there, which meant I had a short reprieve. They were sipping on cans of Colt 45. I kissed them both, threw my coat on an armchair, and grabbed a beer from their six-pack.

There was a tempting smell wafting from the kitchen. "What did you make for dinner, Mama?"

"Meat loaf and scalloped potatoes."

"Mmmm . . . any left?"

"Yeah."

Mama peered at me closely. "What's the matter?"

"Nothing."

Mama spoke directly to Elvira. "Do you believe this chile is gonna sit in that chair and let that lie roll right off her lips?"

In addition to being a gentle and thoughtful woman, Elvira was also tactful. "Now, Mozelle, maybe your daughter has a problem she don't wanna talk about in front of me. I should be runnin' along anyway. It's almost time for *Wheel of Fortune* to come on."

In spite of all my balled-up anger and fear, there was still room in my heart for a lonely old woman who was putting off going to her empty rooms as long as possible. "Oh no, Miss Elvira," I protested, "please stay a while. We can all watch the program together in Mama's room. It'll be good to have company while I eat."

Mama gave me an approving smile and Elvira looked relieved.

The two women gossiped about their neighbors as I bustled about in the kitchen with a cyclone of unanswered questions roaring through my brain. Were Detective Gilchrist and his crew actively looking for someone other than me, or had the videotape and Tiffany Nixon's column persuaded them to stop searching? If I did get arrested, would I have to sit in a filthy jail cell until Keith called in his favors? Why was all this happening to me?

Mama and Elvira whooped and hollered throughout the game show. They played with such intensity, it was as though they were going to win the money themselves. Somehow I knew that Mama was not fooled by my attempts at joining in the hilarity as I shoveled food down my throat without tasting it.

I was right. The door had barely closed on the back of Elvira's heels when she took my wrist in a viselike grip and steered me back to her room.

She looked scared. "What's the matter, Jacqueline?"

"I have something to tell you, but the only reason I'm telling you is that if it does happen, you would read it in the papers and I don't want that." I was babbling and moisture was beading up around my hairline.

"Somethin' bad is gonna happen?" Her eyebrows were furrowed.

"Might happen, Mama . . . might." I patted her folded hands.

"Just tell me," she whispered hoarsely.

I took a deep breath and said it fast. "Keith thinks the police might arrest me for killing Annabelle."

"What?" It was a scream.

It took me almost half an hour to calm her down and explain it all.

After that, warmed by each other's company and united in our fear, Mama and I moseyed through our years together, reminiscing about the high points . . . my junior high school prom which Mama had insisted on attending, to my immense embarrassment . . . my high school graduation ceremony that had run more than an hour beyond schedule because the principal loved to hear himself talk . . . my graduation from the City University where Mama cried so loudly, she could be heard by the candidates crossing the stage to receive their diplomas. There were a few moments of merriment as we recalled my first boyfriend . . . a fifteen-year-old dweeb named Leo who was so afraid of Mama that he perched on the very edge of the sofa whenever he came over. Of course, he finally fell off and hit the floor one evening, and we broke up shortly after that.

We were fine until it was time for us to turn in for the night. Hugging each other, not knowing when I would be taken away or if Keith could really pull another legal miracle out of his hat and bring me back quickly, Mama and I were both overcome with emotion. She wept unashamedly and I bawled like a two-year-old until we tore ourselves apart and I went to lie down in my old room, knowing that both of us would toss and turn until dawn.

I heard sighs, whimpers, and bits of prayer coming from Mama's room all night long and went in several times to rock her frail body back and forth until she went back to sleep.

She was too depressed to get out of bed the next morning. I knew something was wrong when I didn't hear her bustling about right after sunrise. She was just lying there in her bed, eyes wide open, staring at the ceiling.

"Mama, are you all right?"

"No, Jackie. If they lock you up, I ain't never gonna be all right no more."

The dazzling March sunlight flooded her room

through the Venetian blinds and illuminated every wrinkle on her face. When had her cheeks started to sink in? How had all the light fled from her eyes so quickly? She looked very elderly and completely beaten.

"Mama, please don't say that. I'm going to need you by my side to get through this," I whispered hoarsely, attempting to control a sudden fear that my mother might die of heartbreak if she didn't sit up and put her feet on the floor.

21

TIFFANY NIXON STRIKES AGAIN

Paul couldn't believe any of this. I called him as soon as Mama got up and started moving around. He took the day off and spent it at my apartment trying to console me, but I was inconsolable. It didn't help matters that once again, I was the star of Tiffany Nixon's column that morning.

WILL THE LAW APPLY TO BLUE?
by Tiffany Nixon

Ms. Jacqueline Blue has been suspended WITH PAY from her job as senior editor at Welburn Books, Inc., the 100-year-old publishing firm owned by the family of murdered socialite Annabelle Welburn Murray.

Keith Williams, attorney for Ms. Blue, responded with a terse "no comment" when asked about the suspension.

The authors in her care speak very highly of the beautiful and talented Ms. Blue. Hip-hop novelist Jamal Hunt said yesterday, "The only reason why I signed a contract with Welburn Books was to work with Jackie. She fights *hard for Black authors who don't get the same amount of marketing dollars, foreign rights sales, or point-of-sale display units as their white counterparts."*

Celebrated romance writer Willow Van Silver dissolved into tears when told of Ms. Blue's suspension. "I'll take to my bed and not write another word until they bring my beloved Jackie back."

However, an executive at Welburn Books, who prefers to remain unnamed, expressed dismay that the temperamental Ms. Blue has not been arrested. "Although Jackie had a real chip on her shoulder and was constantly getting into fights with people in the industry, I was still shocked to see her on television running away from the murder scene. Why hasn't she been arrested and charged with this terrible crime?"

Why indeed?

We were huddled together in anxiety on my sofa. Paul read the article out loud and then threw the paper across the room. None of it hit the opposite wall. The pages just flew up in the air and fluttered around the room in a black-and-white shower before landing in various places on my pale green carpet.

"What the fuck is her problem?" he screamed in frustration.

The tears streamed down my cheeks and I hugged a cushion tightly to my chest.

Paul gathered me in his arms and rubbed my face gently. "Don't cry, baby," he said. "I'm going to see you through this, no matter what."

But I wasn't crying out of fear that Paul was going to split. I was crying because Tiffany Nixon was the first person who had ever called me "beautiful."

22

VICTOR

I had no intention of just sitting around waiting for the ax to fall on my head. It was time to hit the streets and start doing some detective work. The first thing I did was head back to The Dakota. The doorman, a middle-aged white man with thinning hair, watched my approach with suspicion. I gave him a smile but he remained stoic.

"Sir, my name is Jacqueline Blue."

"I know who you are."

"Okay. What is your name?"

"Walter."

"Walter, I need your help. What happened to Mrs. Murray was terrible but I didn't do it. I figure that someone else she knew and trusted had to enter the building after I left."

"There was only her sister."

I was desperate. "Isn't it possible that you were busy on the phone and someone sneaked past you?"

"Yes, it is possible, but then we'd have that person on the videotape. There was no one."

"Can you think of anything unusual that happened that morning? Something that just doesn't seem to make sense?"

"I'm going to have to ask you to leave, Ms. Blue."

"Please help me."

He picked up the phone. "I'm calling the police."

I fled.

By the following morning, Keith knew all about my visit and he was furious. He was screaming so loudly that I had to pull the phone away from my ear.

"Are you crazy?"

"What do you expect me to do? Sit here until they slap the cuffs on me?"

"I don't care what you do. Take up knitting, go to the gym and hit a punching bag. Whatever. But you stay away from everyone and everything connected with this case."

"Can't I at least talk to Craig about the Moms Mabley book? You said yourself that he didn't do it."

"Jackie, if you can't follow my orders, I will walk off this case and not look back. Do I make myself clear?"

"Yes."

So over the next few days, I spent my time deep cleaning my apartment, holding Mama's hand, and visiting museums and art galleries. My home voicemail system was chock-full of calls from concerned and curious authors, agents, editors, and members of the Black Pack, but I was too depressed to answer their greetings.

Paul usually stopped by after work and stayed until it was time for me to go to bed. I felt guilty that in spite of everything Paul did for me, all of his loving kindness and attempts to make me laugh, I still felt nothing but friendship for him. It occurred to me that I should tell him so and not waste any more of his time (Rosa with the Crooked Nose was getting tired of his neglect and was threatening to kick him to the curb), but my need for someone besides Mama and Elvira to talk to was far too great for me to give him the honesty and consideration he so richly deserved.

It was Paul's idea to have a Black Pack party to lift my spirits. I was lying facedown on my bed as he massaged my back when he brought up the idea.

"Are you crazy? They won't show up because if there is a cameraman outside B. Smith's snapping pictures, they'll catch hell at work," I muttered lazily.

Paul's strong fingers worked my tightened muscles. "I don't care about what happens to them."

"I can't face anybody right now."

"Maybe you could learn something that will help your case. Someone might have overheard vital information that they don't even realize is important."

That made sense to me. "All right, but I still say they won't show up."

Paul stood and rubbed his hands together cheerfully. He'd finally succeeded in giving me hope. "I will get the Black Pack to come."

"How?"

Paul grinned. "By providing guaranteed secrecy, plus free food and booze for them, their spouses, and significant others. We'll have a good time."

Free food? I suddenly knew what he was thinking. "Don't drag poor Richard into this. He is trying to make a go of his new restaurant and feeding all these folks might put a dent in his budget. It isn't fair to your brother."

He knelt on my hardwood bedroom floor and started massaging my bare feet. "Don't worry about Richard. We'll work it out between us."

Paul was going to pay for the party out of his own pocket. I felt it in my gut and I felt a sudden rush of sadness for him. Why couldn't I love this wonderful man?

Keith loved the idea, too, and so, the following Friday evening, the Black Pack meeting was held at Richard's Soul Food Diner.

There was a huge sign on a wooden stand outside the restaurant that said CLOSED FOR PRIVATE PARTY.

Just in case the press had somehow got wind of the gathering, the group waited until dark and then snuck in unobtrusively one by one, at least ten minutes apart.

About twenty people showed up. We all crammed ourselves into a back room that held supplies (I wanted to press my body up against Victor's, but Paul's beady eyes never left me) and didn't speak a word until the last person arrived. That's when Richard locked the front doors, pulled all the blinds and curtains down so it was impossible to see inside, and signaled for the group to come out. It seemed like a very slaves-sneaking-out-the-cabin-to-gather-secretly-in-a-group-down-by-the-creek type of event.

Once we were released, I was enveloped in hugs, kisses, and handshakes before half the group headed for the bar to order drinks and the others to put their belongings in the empty chairs. Since we didn't trust anyone, Richard was going to take food orders, mix drinks, and do all the cooking himself. I would have been beside myself if I were in his shoes, but he looked pleased to be a part of all the intrigue.

I saw Paul fiddling with a CD player that was set up at the end of the bar counter and soon dance tunes from our teenaged years by artists like Rick James, George Clinton, the Brothers Johnson, Kool and The Gang, and Whodini filled the room and Richard's Soul Food Diner began to rock.

Joe sidled up to me.

"Jackie," he said, "I'm so sorry that all this is happening to you."

I felt a pang of dislike at the fascinated expression on Joe's face; it had *tell me all the sordid details* pasted on it. I didn't want to indulge his curiosity so I honed in on Tiffany Nixon's totally unbalanced press coverage. "I've been keeping up with CNN and other papers," I told him. "They are speculating about Annabelle's relationship with her husband and reporting on other mysterious deaths that have occurred in that building since it opened. But Tiffany Nixon is supposed to be my damn sistah and she is not doing any of that."

As I was talking, I became conscious of some other emotion that was flickering around Joe's sober mien. Jealousy. Before I could fully absorb this oddity, Elaine Garner joined us, drink in hand.

"How are you holding up, Jackie?"

"I think half of me is still in shock."

She nodded to show her understanding and played with the swizzle stick. "You ought to fight Tiffany Nixon right back. Get some of the Black activists to protest in front of her offices. If you'd like, I'll give Frank Jenkins a call. He and I have never met, but his cousin Barbara went to Harvard with me."

Frank Jenkins was the fiery leader of a young group that called itself The New Black Warriors. Although I respected their work, I didn't want to turn this whole thing into some horrible media extravaganza that made the networks rich but ended without an answer to the only real question that mattered: Who killed Annabelle, and why?

"No, Elaine, but thanks for the suggestion." Since my publishing career was ruined and I'd probably never see her again after tonight, I wanted to ask her why the fuck she had to mention Harvard every time she opened her mouth, but I restrained myself.

Joe shifted from one foot to the other. "Did Annabelle know about the Black Pack?"

"I doubt it, Joe. If she did, I'm sure she would have mentioned it to me," I answered. "What difference does it make?"

"Just wondering," he mumbled. "I'm going to get some food."

I grabbed him by the arm so hard, he let out a yelp. "Not yet. Why did you ask me that?"

"Jesus! Take it easy," he shouted.

I refused to let go. "Answer me!"

A hand landed on my shoulder. I turned around, and it was Victor. He gave me a slow, sweet smile. The gap between his two front teeth sent me into a lather.

Joe and Elaine skittered away like they were happy to get away from my sudden fit of temper.

"Jackie, it's good to see you."

"Thanks, Victor. Having you all here really lifts my spirits."

He patted my shoulder. "I hope this nightmare ends for you soon."

By now I was practically swooning. Suppose I went to jail in the morning and stayed there for the rest of my life, a victim of a terrible miscarriage of justice, having lost my last chance to go to bed with him? I wouldn't be able to live with myself! And so, the words rushed out. "You know, Victor, I live right around the corner."

He threw back his head and laughed. "Jackie, Jackie, Jackie . . . what am I going to do with you?"

I could think of at least five things that would make the editors of *Playboy* magazine blush but my bold invitation had taken all my energy.

By this point, we were gazing into each other's eyes and my tongue was tied.

He leaned down and whispered into my ear. "Sure, I'll stay with you tonight. But, let's not leave together and start a new round of talk. What's your address?"

I told him.

"Okay. When the party is over, just go home and wait up for me."

How was I going to live through the next three hours? The urge to immediately shove every single one of the seven Black Pack members and their guests out the front door almost overwhelmed me.

Alyssa couldn't even pretend to have a good time. She was crying softly as she hugged me. "Jackie, I just want you to know that I'm in your corner. I have a new job now, and it wouldn't have happened without your help."

I squeezed her back in delight. "So, Pam Silberstein hired you at Hamilton Welsh & Hamilton?"

"Yes, I'm the new senior editor. But Jackie, I don't want to talk about that. Isn't there something I can do to help you out of this crazy situation?"

"Even if there were, Alyssa, I wouldn't let you get involved in this."

She jerked her chin stubbornly. "If you call on me for help, I'll be there. No matter what anyone else thinks about it."

Those were almost the same words I'd said to her such a short time ago, and I had to blink back tears.

"Thanks, Alyssa."

She held onto my arm as I started to move away and looked directly into my eyes. "I'm not letting you go until you promise to keep in touch."

"I promise. By the way, Pam Silberstein is one of the smartest and nicest people I've ever met. Stick with her—she's real cool."

Alyssa nodded and melted into the crowd.

I mingled, joked, and accepted affirmations of faith for a while and then my feet started to hurt so I took a seat at the bar.

"Are you having a good time?" asked Paul, parking himself on the stool beside me.

I crunched a potato chip and nodded. "This is wonderful, Paul. I don't know how to thank you."

He swallowed and cleared his throat. "By staying out of jail. A weekly trip up to Bedford Hills is not how I want to spend the rest of my life."

Bedford Hills was New York State's maximum security prison for women.

There was moisture at the corners of his eyes, so I jabbed him in the stomach to lighten things up. "Oh, come on, Paul. I could write a string of best sellers with that kind of time on my hands."

He laughed. "Yeah. And Elaine Garner could be your editor."

"I'm sure that's what they taught her at Harvard."

He finished the joke. "That's right. Make the money. After all, this is a business."

We giggled like children.

Dallas wandered over. "Seems like the party is really over here in this corner," she grinned. "What's with all the gaiety and merriment?"

Paul filled her in and she whooped with laughter.

"Penelope Aaron can be your agent. All the Black talk she has picked up over the years will come in real handy in the visiting room," Dallas said.

"Those women would kick her ass into infinity if she walked up in there spouting that shit," I said flatly.

Dallas took me by the elbow and whispered in my ear, "I need to talk to you alone."

We excused ourselves and left Paul at the bar.

"What is it, Dallas?"

"Joe Long called me today. He wanted to know if you had ever talked to me about Victor. I had no idea what he was getting at."

"So, what did you say?" I asked calmly.

"I said no and he hung up on me. What did he mean, Jackie?"

A long time ago Dallas caught me up in a real trick bag. What happened was this: The editor-in-chief of *Urban Girl* magazine contacted me, looking for a book deal. She didn't have a definite idea in mind but the circulation of her magazine was over a million. I knew that she had a powerful platform to sell huge numbers of any book she did write. So, I did my homework and came up with a few ideas. At that time, Dallas and I were tight so we went over my list of concepts together. The bitch stabbed me right in the back. The next week I called *Urban Girl* but it was too late. The editor-in-chief had signed with Dallas, who lured her with the ideas that she had stolen from me.

"Dallas, stop fucking around and tell me what you think Joe is up to."

She blinked twice. I stared her down.

"Okay. Haven't you noticed that Joe is always up in Victor's face or trying to imitate him?"

"No."

"Well, he does." Dallas took a sip of her drink. "Joe has a crush on Victor."

I burst out laughing. "Joe is gay?"

Dallas shrugged. "He must be in the closet. I've known him a lot longer than any of you and he has never had a girlfriend. You've been so busy mooning over Victor that you haven't noticed Joe was clocking the brother, too."

"I have not."

Dallas waved away my denial. "Girl, please. Half the fun of the Black Pack meetings is watching your face and Joe's eyes when Victor walks in that door."

I was embarrassed from head to toe.

"Victor is an attractive man but there is nothing going on between us," I said stiffly. "You can tell Joe that if he calls you again."

Dallas nodded without real interest and strolled away in search of juicier gossip.

Finally, it was over.

Paul helped me into my coat. "Come on, I'll walk you home. I may as well crash at your place anyway. I need to help Richard clean this place up first thing in the morning."

I threw the back of my hand against my forehead in an Oscar-winning gesture of despair. "Not tonight, Paul. I really need time alone to think."

He wrapped a scarf around his neck and sucked his teeth. "Girl, you better come on. I'm not trying to stop you from thinking and no way am I riding that subway to Brooklyn tonight if I don't have to."

By now we were out on the sidewalk. He put an arm around my shoulder and we started to walk. I was beginning to get pissed off. Paul was not my man. The man I wanted was coming over. Why should I have to lie and scheme to entertain someone in my own home? When we reached the corner, I stopped.

"Paul, you cannot come home with me tonight. I don't want to talk about it. That's just the way it is."

He looked puzzled. "Did I do something wrong?"

"No. I'll call you tomorrow, okay?" I stood on my tippy-toes to kiss his cheek.

There was hurt and confusion in his face but he kissed me back and crossed the street toward the subway.

Oh, God. It was like beating up on Bambi.

I practically ran around the corner. The apartment was tidy but I had to change the sheets, the towels, and find something seductive to wear. It had been so long since I'd been to bed with a man—five years and three days at last count—that there were no teddies, lacy stockings, or garters in my wardrobe.

I took a hasty shower, almost scalding myself in the process, toweled myself off and bumped my toe painfully on my way out of the bathroom. "Ow!"

Naked, I ransacked my bureau and closets. The best I could do was a black slip with no panties on. After dashing on far too much *White Diamonds* perfume, I was ready. Except I wasn't. Not really. I paced the floor in black stiletto heels, wringing my hands. Suppose he was used to thin women and I was too fat? Would he groan and collapse with a hernia while trying to lift me? On top of that, I had come on to him like a Penthouse Pet, and now he was probably expecting a superstar performance from me between the sheets. Worse, suppose he wanted oral sex? The only time I had ever done it was in my fantasies. I might bite down on him too hard, causing a terrible, gaping, bloody wound in his penis that would take twelve stitches to close!

By the time the downstairs doorbell rang, I was in such a state that I needed a drink to calm down but there was no time to get one.

I stepped to the intercom box to answer the summons. My mouth was dry as I pushed the TALK button. "Who is it?"

"Me."

I buzzed him in, patted my hair, slid my hands down the sides of my body, and glided toward the front door. There was a knock. I unlocked the door, released the security chain, and there stood Paul.

I was shocked and alarmed. "What are you doing here?"

His eyes were hard and flat. His moustache quivered beneath his nose. His body was rigid. The arms held tightly against his torso with the hands balled into fists. When he opened his mouth to speak, it was like watching a trapdoor unlock.

"Is this the outfit you wear for deep thinking?" he sneered.

"Paul, I . . ."

He cut me off. "Don't bother making up another lie. The next time you're in trouble, call Victor."

He gave my trampy little outfit a withering glance and fled back down the stairs. I closed the door and rummaged around in my kitchen cupboards for a half-empty bottle of rum that I'd left there a long time ago.

My hands were trembling. I turned the bottle up to my lips and took a long swallow. The liquid burned its way down to my nervous stomach.

Feeling better, I decided not to worry about Paul until morning. I would call him then and say the right words that would turn us into friends again. Yes, I was wrong for lying to him but he had no right to pull the jealous shit that he'd done. He just needed time to cool off and he'd be able to see that.

I placed the bottle on the coffee table along with a bucket of ice and a liter of Pepsi. I dimmed the lights and put a Maxwell CD on the stereo to complete the seduction scene. I had just repaired my lipstick when the downstairs doorbell rang again.

This time it was Victor.

He eyed me appreciatively as I took his coat and hung it up. "My, don't you look delicious."

We settled in on my sofa, drinking and talking shop until Victor raised the subject of Annabelle's murder.

"So, have there been any new developments in the police investigation?"

"I don't know. Why would they share anything with me?"

He crossed one leg over the other. "It just seems like someone had to see something on the morning it happened. Maybe something very important that didn't mean anything at the time."

"Maybe I should hire a hypnotist to refresh my memory," I replied playfully.

"That's a great idea, Jackie. You could . . ."

I cut him off there and moved in closer. "Victor, we can talk about murder tomorrow morning if you want to, okay?"

There was nothing else to say. It was time to DO, and we both knew it.

The silence grew uncomfortable, and I wondered

why he didn't make a move. He drummed his fingers on the coffee table and hummed along to the music until I was about to shake him like a rag doll.

I stood up, placed my hands on my hips, and gave him a seductive smile.

"What's going on?" he asked.

Stand your punk ass up, is what I wanted to say.

I was exasperated beyond belief. "Victor, what part of 'there is a healthy woman wearing a thin slip with nothing on underneath, staring at you with lust in her heart' don't you get?"

He coughed. "Do you want to lay down?"

No, you dumb fuck. I want to play ice hockey.

"Yes," I said sweetly.

This was definitely not my dream encounter. The brother was turning out to be less Richard Roundtree in *Shaft* and more Jethro in *The Beverly Hillbillies*. His behavior was unfathomable . . . either he was gay, stupid, or had a tiny little weenie that he was too embarrassed to show me. My crush on Victor Bell was fading.

"Lead the way," he said.

All the lights in my bedroom were off but we could see each other in silhouette by the light streaming in from the hallway.

There wasn't much in the way of foreplay but I didn't really care. Victor's unclothed body was magnificent. He pulled the straps of the slip and I wriggled out of it. Gently, he pressed me back on the bed and hovered above me on his knees, licking my breasts, shoulders, stomach. His muscles rippled every time he moved. I pulled him around the waist and our bodies melded together.

"Victor, Victor!" My breathing was ragged and my pulse was racing.

He made a sudden move with his hand and the framed picture of me, Annabelle, and Denzel fell off my nightstand. It hit the hardwood floor and the glass made a little clink sound as it broke. Victor murmured, "I'm sorry," as he reached over me and picked it up. He looked at the picture and groaned. His erection deflated.

I took the picture from his hand and threw it across the room. "Don't worry about it. I'll get a new frame."

He nodded and stroked himself for a few seconds as I kissed him all over the face and chest.

"It's not working," Victor replied desperately.

And "it" certainly wasn't. I reached down and touched his dick. It was as limp as a used dishrag.

He pushed me off him and lay flat on his back. "I'm sorry."

Concealing my frustration, I pulled the sheet over our nakedness and put some pep into my voice. "The night is young, handsome. Don't worry about it."

"Forget it, Jackie." He sounded disappointed.

I laid my head on his chest and my fingers played in his pubic hair. He lay still as stone. "Victor?"

"Yes?"

"Would you kiss me?"

He gathered me up in his strong arms and pressed his lips to mine. That wasn't good enough for me. I managed to part them and stuck my tongue right into his warm mouth. All of a sudden, Victor tossed the sheets aside and leaped from my bed. I watched miserably as his perfect body ran away from me and into the bathroom. I could hear him retching and coughing through the closed door.

This was a nightmare and I had no one to blame but myself. I had pulled out every trick in the book to gain Victor's interest and he had let me know in every way possible that he was not interested. Now he had touched me and the experience was making him throw up. I pulled the covers up to my chin and just lay there with my eyes closed, not knowing what else to do.

There was the sound of running water—he was rinsing the taste of my tongue and the vomit from his mouth.

Tears stung the back of my eyelids and I'd never felt uglier or more worthless in my whole life.

I sat up when Victor came out of the bathroom. "Are you all right?" I asked politely.

He started putting his clothes on without looking me in the eye. "No. I'm not feeling well so it's best if I go home."

Even though I had finally gotten Victor out of my system and only wanted him to leave, he was still a sick guest in my home and Mama had raised me right. "Do you want something to settle your stomach . . . Maalox, Alka Seltzer?"

"Thanks, but no."

There was nothing left to say.

23

BLACK FINGERTIPS

JACKIE HAD WIFE SINGING THE BLUES
by Tiffany Nixon

Once a mistress, always a mistress?

Hank St. John and Jacqueline Blue met at City College on 135th Street. Sparks flew and soon the pretty college senior and her very married English professor were dating. It didn't take long for Miss Blue to become dissatisfied with the stolen moments, clandestine meetings, and lonely holidays that have enraged mistresses since the beginning of time. Miss Blue began to demand more. Mr. St. John, afraid of losing her, complied.

Eventually, Mrs. St. John got wind of the affair and confronted her husband. She demanded that he cease and desist or she would leave, taking their three children with her.

Professor St. John went to Miss Blue's apartment, which was located a few blocks from the campus, to deliver news which Ms. Blue did not want to hear: the relationship was over.

Mrs. St. John says, "Jacqueline Blue began following me around, threatening to steal the children, and gener-

*ally made my life hell until we moved to Long Island a
year later."*

*According to my sources at Welburn Books, Ms. Blue,
who is now a decade older, had a "very close" relationship with Annabelle Welburn's husband.*

Did Jackie covet Craig?

Keith demanded my side of the story. As I told him, I
didn't know that Hank was married until we had already
started sleeping together. It is true that I should have
ended our relationship as soon as I learned the truth,
but by that time I was in love with him. When he came
to see me, looking all sad, I knew what was going on before he told me. I gave him a kiss good-bye and disappeared from his life. I did not harass his wife, call his
home, or threaten to take his children. Why would I, a
twenty-two-year-old girl with no job lined up and only
three weeks away from graduation, want to steal some
kids that I had no way of feeding?

Mama called. "What is this mess about you havin' sex
with some married man?"

"It was a long time ago, Mama," I answered wearily.

"How could you do somethin' like that? You was
raised better."

"I'm sorry."

"Didn't you care about his wife and kids?" Mama
sounded angry and disappointed.

"I was young, Mama."

"Don't you give me that bullshit, Jacqueline Blue.
Married is married, and you knew that. Sell it to the
damned jury."

I figured Mama was putting me in the same whorish
category as the woman who ran off with Daddy, and my
spirits sank to a new low.

She hung up before I could say another word and
never mentioned it again.

I was furious. Why was Tiffany Nixon digging around in my past? Would her own background stand up under such intense scrutiny?

Two weeks later, a grand jury returned an indictment against me. As a result, my employment at Welburn Books was officially terminated, and I was thrown off the payroll. Alyssa was the only member of the Black Pack who called to sympathize but I was too upset to talk to her. It was a bitter pill for me to swallow.

One evening, I was watching the six o'clock news when Keith called to say that there was a big problem we needed to talk about and he was coming over to my place.

I was wearing a gray sweat suit, sneakers, and no makeup but I didn't care. Paul had not answered any of my phone calls since the night of my disastrous encounter with Victor and other journalists had united with Tiffany Nixon in a thunderous cry for my blood. My life didn't seem worth living and I was so depressed that it took me a while to even wonder why Keith was coming to Harlem instead of summoning me to his office.

I'd had more than enough time to mull over the grimy details of Annabelle's unfortunate demise. Stitching them all together, it was clear to me that the doorman, someone who lived in The Dakota, Craig, or Annabelle's sister had committed the terrible act. I was still concerned about staying out of prison, but that wasn't enough anymore. I wanted to clear my name more than anything else and the only way that could happen was if the killer was caught, convicted, and thrown into jail.

The three-family town house that I lived in faced a tree-lined street of brownstones, some of them valued at over two million dollars in this new Harlem, which was becoming more overpriced by the day. Restlessly, I turned off the television set and stood looking out my front window, peering at the elegant homes through the pouring rain and wondering if I'd ever have enough money to buy one.

I was imagining myself as the wife of a handsome, well-to-do gentleman living blissfully in one of the buildings with our two beautiful children (a boy and a girl) when the buzzer rang.

Keith shrugged out of his coat and folded it neatly over a chair. He was wearing a black suit, crisp burgundy shirt, and a black tie that had swirls of a maroon design in it. "Jackie, you need to sit down. I have bad news."

We sat down on the sofa.

"I don't really know how to tell you this," he said.

My apartment suddenly felt cold, even though the thermostat was turned way up.

"Just tell me, Keith, and get it over with."

He put his arm around me and drew my face down on his chest. "The grand jury returned an indictment and a warrant has been issued for your arrest, Jackie. I promised that you would surrender quietly within the next two hours. I didn't want Detective Gilchrist showing up here with reporters on his heels and dragging you out in handcuffs in front of your neighbors."

I couldn't focus on Keith's face. The living room was tilting slightly and the sofa seemed to be revolving at an impossible angle.

"This is insane," I yelled. "If you hadn't kept my hands tied up like this, I could have done my own research and we'd have other suspects by now!"

"Jackie, calm down."

"Don't tell me to calm down! I trusted you and now I'm going to jail!"

"It doesn't mean you're going to be convicted of this murder. The state still has to prove its case but the district attorney is under a lot of pressure and felt he had to set a wheel in motion."

"Keith, I don't give a fuck about all that right now. I have to spend tonight in police custody and it's all your fault."

"Jackie, I couldn't allow you to run all over town asking questions. You might have said or done something that would jeopardize this case when it finally gets to court. Worse, you might have panicked the killer and ended up in the morgue. Now, you've got to keep trusting me even when things look bad. Okay?"

"Suppose you're wrong? Suppose I end up in the penitentiary?"

"The evidence against you is all circumstantial and I'll make sure that we get a jury which understands the concept of reasonable doubt."

Circumstantial evidence. A jury. Reasonable doubt. Even after all that had happened, it still seemed unbelievable. "Mama," I managed to gasp.

"Call her, Jackie. Don't let her hear this on the news."

I dialed the number and as soon as Mama answered, I started crying so hard that Keith had to take the phone from me and tell her himself. "Mrs. Blue, please calm down . . . It's just for two nights. Jackie can post bail on Monday and . . . How much? . . . I really don't know."

How much, indeed. Evidently Keith had not given any thought to that question because his head suddenly slumped to his chest.

My heart was thumping noisily enough to wake a long-dead corpse; I was panting for breath and had to force myself to inhale and puff the air out normally; my visual perception lessened to a maximum of two feet before me. I was trembling with fear, and my head felt like there was a steel vise clamped to the back of it. Suddenly, there was only one voice I wanted to hear.

"I've got to get in touch with Paul."

The next time you're in trouble, call Victor.

Had he really meant those words? Was he angry that I had been too much of a coward to call after our fight?

Keith waited patiently as I dialed the number. My hands were shaking and as soon as he answered, a wail came from somewhere deep in my soul.

"Paul, they're charging me with Annabelle's murder!"

"What?" It was a gasp.

"Keith is here and he's taking me to jail."

"Put him on the phone."

I passed the receiver to Keith and sobbed as my lawyer explained the situation. Before we left the apartment, Paul got back on the line and promised that he'd move heaven and earth to get me out as quickly as possible.

There was a black, chauffeur-driven limousine parked right in front of my building. The driver jumped out with an umbrella to protect us from the thunderstorm and opened the back door. The partition was kept closed all the way downtown so that the driver couldn't hear what was said.

Keith patted my hand. "Everything is going to be all right. Is there anyone you want me to call for you?"

"If you'll just check in on my mother every few hours until I get back, that'll be enough."

Keith cleared his throat. "I don't mean to be insensitive, Jackie, but you really need to concentrate on raising that bail money."

"Paul said he will help me."

"What if he can't? You need a Plan B."

I knew a lot of rich authors and agents but not well enough to hit them up for a couple of thousand dollars. "I can't think of anyone else," I whispered.

"What about one of your girlfriends?"

I didn't have any girlfriends. Not a single one. Mama

had preached to me so long and decisively about the folly of having females in your house and your business that I'd never really trusted members of my own sex.

It wasn't until after I moved out and Mama got lonely that she allowed herself a girlfriend, even though Elvira had lived across the hall from us for almost twenty years.

"There is no one like that in my life," I whispered.

Keith sighed. "I spoke to the district attorney just before I picked you up. We both agreed that since this is Saturday night, it is a lot easier to get you in without the media getting wind of it."

I knew that Keith was just trying to keep me from having a nervous breakdown. He was wasting his time. It wasn't the press that had me terrified. "Are they going to lock me in a cell?"

The limousine turned up Adam Clayton Powell Boulevard, headed for 125th Street.

"Not exactly. It's a holding pen. We're skipping the whole precinct thing and taking you straight to Central Booking."

His tone suggested that I should be impressed with the enormous clout he wielded with the powers-that-be. Since I didn't know what "the whole precinct thing" was and what indignities would have awaited me there, I was unmoved. I focused on "holding pen" and an image of a huge basketball court-type space surrounded by razor wire fixed itself in my mind and I started to hyperventilate. Keith grabbed me by the back of the neck, forcing my head down.

"Put your head between your knees and take deep breaths," he ordered.

The interior of the plush vehicle was silent as I huffed and puffed loudly. Then I noticed the fully stocked bar. "Keith, I need a drink."

"No!" shouted Keith. "I don't want liquor on your breath."

"Don't be an asshole, Keith. I'm about to faint."

We went at it, bickering like an old married couple or a bunch of siblings as I breathed in and out between my sweatpant-clad thighs, with one hand reaching up wildly for a drink of anything alcoholic.

I won and by the time we were headed down the West Side Highway, I had gulped two shot glasses of straight whiskey. Keith gave me some orange Tic-Tacs to cover the smell. When I had recovered enough to lie back against the expensive leather and stretch my legs out, Keith held my hand and spoke quietly.

"Jackie, I need you to be brave. Do you hear me?"

I nodded, unable to speak.

"When we get downtown, you will be relieved of all your belongings, fingerprinted, photographed, and then taken to a holding area. I can't come with you but when they bring you into the courtroom for arraignment on Monday morning, I'll be right there waiting for you, understand?"

"Monday! This is Saturday night! "Oh Keith, isn't there a night court or something that could spring me before tomorrow morning?"

He patted my knee. "I'm so sorry, Jackie. That doesn't work in a murder case."

"What is an arraignment?"

"An arraignment is the first appearance in court before a judge on a criminal charge. The charges against you will be read or you will be asked if you are aware of the charges against you, and you will be asked how you wish to plead."

The limousine sped through the dark, wet streets, and with each roll of the tires, I felt another crumbling of who I was and what I used to be.

The car finally stopped in front of a fortress-like building. As Keith helped me out, I noticed that a lot of police cars were parked on the street. Detective Marcus

Gilchrist stepped from the shadows. Keith pushed me in back of him and had a whispered discussion which I could not hear.

I just stood in the rain. Part of me felt removed from the whole scene. Surely this was some other woman's life I was watching on a movie screen—in some surrealistic plot created by Hollywood writers. It just didn't make sense that a person could really get entangled in the criminal justice system on the most serious of all charges just by misplacing an appointment book and running across a lobby! Why, the whole thing was insane and getting crazier by the moment. It was time for me to leave this mess—yeah, that was it. All I had to do was hail a cab and go to Mama's house. I must have turned to leave because there was a sudden pain in my arm.

"Stop it," Keith whispered in my ear through gritted teeth. "If you run, it's all over. You'll never get bail if you're pegged as a flight risk."

"Ow," was my reply. His hands had clamped down on me like a vise. "Let go of my arm."

"Shut up and don't move."

He turned back around and continued his conversation with Gilchrist.

At that moment I realized that I was a prisoner. This was no movie and no one in the stone building in front of me cared about the famous restaurants I was in the habit of going to, the fancy names and addresses on my Rolodex, how Mama was home crying her eyes out, the fact that my career was going up in smoke, or that I really didn't commit the crime.

Suddenly Detective Gilchrist pulled me away from Keith and the two of us were walking toward the entrance. I twisted my neck around to look for Keith. He was just standing there, making no attempt to shield himself from the rain that was pouring down on him.

"Keep your head up, Jackie," he shouted.

I could tell by the tone of his voice that the expression on my face must have been suicidal. Gilchrist didn't say a word as he held the door open and led me into his world.

It was a great, big room with no windows, lots of cops, a few desks scattered about, several partitions, and a counter with a bored-looking officer behind it. As we approached the counter, I realized that there was one gigantic cell built into the left side of the room which held women and another on the right which held men.

The law of Karma had to be working here, but what on earth had I ever done to deserve this? Was this payback for the $25 I'd lifted from Mama's purse when I was in high school and then swore I knew nothing about the missing money? The abortion I'd had in freshman year? The married man I'd had an affair with ten years ago?

An old Black man was holding on to the bars and screaming over and over again "I'm Smokey Robinson, goddammit. Get me Berry Gordy!"

I felt Gilchrist nudging me forward, and then we were at the counter. Gilchrist handed some papers to the cop with one hand and held my arm with the other.

The cop looked at me. "What is your name?"

"Jacqueline Blue."

"Address?"

"125 West 111th Street. Harlem."

"Age?"

"Thirty-two."

"Any previous arrests?"

"No."

"Okay. Place your personal belongings on the counter."

I put my Kate Spade tote bag on the space in front of him.

He unzipped it and named each item out loud as he

pulled it from the case and wrote it down on a form. "Keys . . . wallet . . . book . . . lipstick . . . pen . . . pink case."

He shook the "pink case" in my face. "What is in this case?"

My voice was trembling. "It's Fashion Fair Perfect Finish Foundation."

He blinked. "What?"

"Ma . . . Makeup," I stuttered.

Gilchrist released my arm. "Ted, let me see the book."

So, the cop's name was Ted.

The "book" was my Filofax.

Ted handed it over—Gilchrist leafed through its pages, grunting in satisfaction. "This is evidence. I'm gonna hang on to it."

Ted frowned and snatched it back. "You know better than that. Go through channels."

Gilchrist cursed under his breath and marched me across the room to one of the partitions. There was a white woman inside wearing navy pants and a white shirt with some kind of shiny silver badge on it. She was seated high on a stool with her arm resting on a camera which stood on a tripod.

She smiled at the detective. "Hey, Marc. What's new?"

He gave her a friendly slap on the back. "Lena, I'm so tired, I could curl up and fall asleep right here on this floor."

"I know the feelin'."

She gestured to me. "Stand over there, right on the X."

There was a huge, black "X" painted on the floor about three feet away from her.

She gave me a piece of black plastic with numbers on

it. "Hold that in front of your chest." She aimed the camera at me. *Snap.* "Turn right." *Snap.* "Now left." *Snap.*

By the time my mug shot was done and I had been searched, tears were sliding down my face again and Gilchrist seemed uncomfortable. "You got a good lawyer, Miss Blue. This coulda been a lot worse. Let's just get the fingerprinting over with and then you can sit down. Follow me."

He didn't grab my arm this time, trusting me not to make a break for the door. I trudged behind him, wishing that a stray bullet would hit me and end my life. Anything would be better than this scorching, searing shame.

A weary cop who looked way past retirement age pressed each one of my fingers onto a black, inky pad and then onto different, previously marked squares of a white, cardboard sheet. Afterward, Gilchrist gave me some tissue to wipe off my black fingertips.

That was it.

For as long as the criminal justice system existed, there would be a record of the fact that on April 12, 1997, Jacqueline Blue was arrested and booked on a charge of second-degree murder.

When we reached the immense holding cell for females which was stuffed with women of all sizes, shapes, and colors, I balked like a stubborn mule. The commotion in there was deafening and the bench that ringed the wall was occupied, leaving the majority of the prisoners standing in the middle of the floor or leaning against the bars. The cop who was standing in front of it pulled out a ring of keys.

"You can't put me in there." I clung to Gilchrist desperately.

He sighed. "I don't have a choice, Miss Blue."

A key went in the door.

I racked my brain frantically and then took my best shot. "My face has been all over the papers. Don't you have protective custody? Keith Williams will raise hell from here to the Supreme Court if I get one scratch on me!"

At the sound of his name, all of the women got real quiet. Both Gilchrist and the cop with the keys stopped moving. Each one looked at the other. Both wanted to throw me in the cell; neither wanted the responsibility if something went wrong and everyone in earshot knew I spoke the truth.

"Does she fit the definition of celebrity?" asked the cop.

Gilchrist scratched his head. "I don't know, but I'm getting off in an hour so put her in the back. If Hap doesn't like it when he comes on duty, let him throw her in here with the population."

I didn't know who "Hap" was, but I doubted he wanted the responsibility of my demise, either.

Gilchrist walked away. "See you in court," he flung at me over his shoulder.

The cop yanked me by the arm down the hallway and away from the mass of women who had resumed their noisy, incomprehensible babble.

24

A PRIVATE SPACE

Since night court is for those accused of petty crimes and there is no court on Sundays, I spent two nights in solitary confinement at Central Booking. My cell was small but at least I didn't have to share it. There was a bench to sleep on and a toilet. I lost all sense of night and day because the only light came from a small bulb suspended from the ceiling.

That first night, I simply sat on the hard bench, trying to watch every corner of the cell. Suppose there was a hole with rats in it, waiting for me to close my eyes so they could come out and start gnawing at my face, hands, arms? I screamed aloud in fright at the thought of it. Then I started thinking about what happened to Abner Louima. Suppose a sadistic cop came in and raped me with a broomstick. Sweat poured down my face as I imagined that scene. "Oh, Mama, Mama, Mama," I moaned. I had no way to defend myself and even Keith wouldn't be able to help me as I was assaulted. A female officer came to the cell as the scene with the broomstick played itself out in my head. She was holding a small paper plate and a cup. "You hungry?" she asked with a smile.

"No!" I shrieked. "Stay out!"

The smile disappeared and she shrugged. "Suit yourself."

The noise from the general holding pens continued. There were no distinct words or sentences. Just a constant, earsplitting rumble followed by intermittent sounds of weeping and other signs of misery. I sat on that bench for hours with my back against the wall, my knees drawn up to my chin and my arms wrapped around them, too scared to move. The pressure on my bladder was intense but I didn't want to pull down my panties and sweatpants to use the toilet. I didn't want to give someone with a broomstick any ideas. Finally, the dam burst and I peed right where I sat.

The next night was a tiny bit better. I still wouldn't pull down my clothes or accept any food because I didn't want the door to open but I had begun to hate everyone who had a hand in sending me to jail. I alternated between pacing my cell and dozing fitfully on the urine-damp bench—planning, plotting, and hating.

The first thing I had to do was wipe any feelings of self-pity from my mind until the real murderer was exposed. Next, I had to take charge of my own case. No matter what Keith Williams said about letting him handle everything, there was no way I was going to do that. His job was to find a case for reasonable doubt and keep me out of Bedford Hills. I wanted more. I wanted my name cleared and if the police weren't going to look for the murderer, I would do it myself.

And then there was Miss Nixon.

I hated Tiffany Nixon.

If it were not for her horrible columns, the district attorney would not have been under so much pressure from politicians and the public to lock me up.

I knew her type.

What she had done to me was not personal. It was to

curry favor with the dominant culture and win her a prize for outstanding crime reporting if I was indicted and brought to trial. Whether I was convicted or not, she would forever be known as the Black reporter who didn't let any sense of racial solidarity get in the way of her duties to the entity which paid her. Such a label for a Black professional in any industry was as good as gold when it was time for prizes and promotions.

But she wasn't going to get away with it unless I was held without bail and sent away to prison without ever walking the streets of New York again.

That meant I had to get out and Paul was just one egg in a real shaky basket. The police owed me a phone call and I decided to use it to call Elaine Garner.

If Paul didn't come through and she could find a way to get me out, I would start feeding her the inside story on my relationship with the dead heiress, Keith Williams, the murder investigation, and my unauthorized search for a killer. It was a guaranteed best-seller that she might be able to use to leverage herself into a publisher's chair. The tiny number of people who held those seats wielded a tremendous amount of power. It was they who ultimately decided which manuscripts the editors were allowed to buy and turn into books.

No African-American had ever held one of those seats at a major publishing house. Maybe Elaine would be the first.

What could be more Harvard than that?

25

PAUL

I finally reached the courtroom for arraignment on Monday morning. I was conscious of being led out of the darkness of my cell into a brightly lit courtroom where men and women in conservative business suits were running to and fro waving sheaves of paper at the judge.

There were rows of people seated, anxiety on their faces, watching the door I'd just emerged from. There was a wooden bar separating the prisoners from their audience. Mama, Keith, and Paul were sitting in the front row, and I waved to show my awareness of their presence.

A clerk called my name and Keith's, plus a string of sentences that were legalese for second-degree murder. Keith stepped up to the plate. He was wearing a different Armani suit than the sodden one I had last seen him in. He looked smooth and dapper.

The judge asked me, "How do you plead, Ms. Blue?"

"Not guilty," I replied.

Keith gave my hand a reassuring squeeze.

A very tall, painfully thin woman who looked like Olive Oyl gave me a look of disgust and a flash of the

Thin Pink Line as she joined us in front of the judge. As she presented her case against bail, I realized that her name was Ruth Champ and she was from the district attorney's office.

Champ said, "Your Honor, this was a vicious, unprovoked crime. The defendant has wealthy associates and that makes her a significant flight risk. I hereby request a denial of bail in this case."

Keith responded in a voice laced with sarcasm. "Your Honor, this is absolutely ridiculous. My client was born and raised in this city. She has an elderly mother here who is her only family. What is more, the case against my client is entirely circumstantial and without any merit. My client does not have a secret trunk of gold hidden somewhere that can yield enough money to set up some luxurious lifestyle in another country at the drop of a hat. I hereby request that my client be released on her own recognizance."

Champ hissed. "No bail? That would be outrageous."

The judge held up a hand to silence them both and set bail at $250,000.

I looked around for Elaine Garner, but she was nowhere in the room.

Keith pulled me aside. "This is wonderful."

"Wonderful? I don't have $250,000!"

"You only need ten percent of that amount to walk out of this courtroom, and Paul Dodson has agreed to put up his home as collateral."

I glanced over my shoulder and saw that Mama was sitting alone. "Where is he?"

"Paul had to go downstairs and sign some paperwork. As soon as that is done, you'll be free to go."

"Can I go sit with Mama? She looks terrible."

Keith patted my shoulder. "It'll just be a few more minutes, Jackie. You can't leave this area of the courtroom until Paul's work is done."

In other words, I was still a prisoner.

"Will you go and sit with her, then? She looks so lost and scared."

"Sure."

And then I was alone, watching the next defendants as they were brought in to stand quaking before the judge, but my thoughts were on Paul. He had schemed, saved, begged, and borrowed to purchase that house. It was his pride and joy, but he had put it up on the block for me. No one except Mama had ever trusted or loved me that much, and I couldn't stop the tears from streaming from my eyes.

It took close to an hour for the paperwork to go through and my personal belongings found and returned to me, but finally, I was free.

As I hugged Mama, who clutched me like she would never let go, I was extremely sensitive to the fact that I smelled like jail. Paul and Keith stood off to the side, smiling at us, until I was able to pry Mama's arms away.

Paul gave me a hug and whispered, "It's really good to see you, Jackie," into my ear.

"I don't know how to thank you, Paul," I whispered back.

"We'll talk later," he murmured.

The four of us locked arms and walked out onto Centre Street, where reporters converged on us like a pack of wild dogs.

"Did you kill your boss, Jackie?"

"Hey Jackie, look this way!"

"Who is paying for Keith Williams?"

"Is that your boyfriend, Jackie? Is he standing by you?"

"Why'd you do it, Jackie? What was the motive?"

"Are you in love with Craig Murray?"

"Who is the old lady? Is that your mother?"

"Who killed Annabelle Murray?"

Keith had been prepared for this scene. Two rows of

police officers held the journalists and their flashbulb-popping news crews away from us as Keith, his mouth tight, pushed us toward his waiting limousine.

Jamal Hunt was standing next to the car. He pushed past Keith and hugged me. The cameras flashed away. "Jackie, I know you're not guilty and I'm praying for you!" he yelled.

I whispered my thanks and climbed into the limo. As the car pulled away from the curb, I saw the reporters rush toward Jamal, who promptly held a hardcover book above his head so the cover would appear in all the papers. Using my predicament to promote his current novel was a tasteless, selfish, and totally unforgivable act and, for just a second, I was glad that I'd lost my job so I wouldn't have to deal with him.

Mama leaned back against the plush upholstery. Her face looked ashen.

It would have been stupid to ask if she were all right, so I just held her hand and said nothing. The air suddenly filled up with the briny scent of stale piss, but no one mentioned it.

"Let's get out of here. I need to go home and change clothes."

"You can't go home," Keith told me. "The police tore the place up, looking for evidence. Besides, the media knows where you live now and they'll be camped outside until the trial is over."

I couldn't take any more. "Where am I supposed to live, for God's sake?" It was a scream.

Mama patted my hand. "Shush, baby. Put your stuff in storage and come stay with me."

"I want to go home!" I was yelling and pounding my fists on the seat like a two-year-old.

Paul pulled my head onto his chest. "You're always welcome at my place."

"No. I need to know that Jackie is safe," Keith said

firmly. "I have a place down in Greenwich Village. There isn't much furniture, but she needs to stay there until this is all over."

There is something about being arrested, finger-printed, and photographed and then wearing the same panties for forty-eight hours that can put a woman in a really foul mood. "I'm going home as soon as I can, but take me to Mama's for right now."

"Fine," he replied. He slid back the partition and gave new instructions to the driver and then picked up a newspaper that was lying on the seat. The headline blared, *HARLEM WOMAN CHARGED IN EXECUTIVE'S DEATH.*

It was the *Comet.* I snatched it from his hand, causing Mama to give me a look that said *you were raised better.* I did-n't care. I had just emerged from the bowels of hell and my manners would not return until there was a decent plate of food in front of me and some clean clothes on my body.

HARLEM WOMAN CHARGED IN EXECUTIVE'S DEATH
by Roy Breyer

A Welburn Books editor was arrested on Saturday after police said she strangled her employer, Annabelle Welburn, to death three months ago.

Jacqueline Blue, 32, of Harlem was charged with sec-ond-degree murder.

"It was just senseless. Senseless and needless," Man-hattan District Attorney Darryl Givan said at a press conference.

According to Givan, Ms. Blue cornered Welburn in the vestibule of her eighth-floor penthouse and the two argued over a job promotion that had been denied Miss Blue. Enraged, Miss Blue forced the beautiful, blond pub-lisher into a bathroom, where the vicious attack took *place. If convicted, Blue could be sentenced to life in prison without possibility of parole.*

His story was only one of many on the subject, but I didn't read the rest. Even though the charges were false, I took some comfort in the fact that Mr. Breyer had simply reported the events as they were told to him—unlike the vicious attacks that were Ms. Nixon's specialty.

I gave the paper back to Keith and didn't say another word all the way to Hell's Kitchen.

There was a knot of journalists and photographers waiting in front of Mama's building when Keith's limousine pulled up. Worse, her neighbors were talking to them. What stories were they telling about me? That I once fell off the monkey bars and skinned my knee on the ground? That I had cheated my classmate, a tiny Chinese boy named Weng Loo, out of fifteen cents when we were in the third grade? That Mama wouldn't make friends with any of the women on the block because she distrusted all females? That I almost got hit by a car while dashing across the street to buy a popsicle when I was ten? What were they saying that caused the journalists to nod up and down as seriously as though they were listening to a scientist explain the cure for cancer?

"How did they know I would come here?" I whispered.

Keith sighed. "They didn't. But your mother had to come home sooner or later. I'll bet they're willing to pay her a lot of money just for a few photos and stories of your childhood."

"I ain't got nuthin' to say to those people," Mama declared.

Keith rubbed his chin. "Actually, I think you should talk to them—we need public sympathy for Jackie. So far, the only photo they have seen is the video of her running across the lobby. Tomorrow morning her mug shot will be on the cover of every major newspaper in the country. Jackie desperately needs someone to balance that image."

Mama looked bewildered. "What do you want me to tell 'em?"

"Just the truth, Mrs. Blue."

The pack turned away from the common people and surrounded the limousine. Since the windows were tinted, they couldn't see inside.

"This is absolutely incredible," Paul said.

Keith grimaced. "There is probably three times this number outside Jackie's place, and they'll be there every day until the juice has been totally sucked from this story. Even worse, someone looking to get famous might take a shot at her. She can't go home or stay here."

The lump in my throat wouldn't allow me to respond.

He slid the partition back and gave orders to the driver. "Mrs. Blue and I are getting out here. Take Jackie and her friend downtown to the apartment and then come back for me later." He carefully removed three keys from a ring and gave them to me.

Mama folded her arms across her chest. "Nobody is gonna run me outta my own house."

"I can't leave her here alone," I said.

Keith shook his head. "The situation will just be a daily nuisance for your mother but you are in real danger. I won't allow you to stay here." He paused with his hand on the door handle. "Are you ready, Mrs. Blue?"

"Yes."

Mama and I hugged each other and then Keith opened the door. I clutched the keys to my hiding place in my palm.

Paul looked dazed, and although he held my hand tightly, neither of us was in the mood for conversation.

The only thought which swirled through my mind on the way downtown was that I'd buy a gun and kill myself before allowing anyone to lock me in a jail cell again.

My hideout was a three-story brownstone near Houston Street. When the driver parked in front of it, I asked, "Which floor am I going to?"

He laughed. "This whole building is Mr. Williams's place. You can live in any room you want."

I dragged my tired body up the steps. My life in Harlem was on hold. This new home in Greenwich Village was only temporary. What was going to become of me?

It was an elegant, twelve-room residence with high ceilings, decorative molding, hardwood floors, huge French windows, and a back garden. There was a grand piano in the first-floor living room with a four-foot stack of Keith's autobiography, *Winner*, standing next to it, a round wooden table with four chairs in the huge, eat-in kitchen, and a fully furnished bedroom on the second floor. Otherwise, the place was bare.

Was this where Keith brought his one-night stands? It certainly seemed that way. I couldn't help laughing at Keith's setup, and the sound echoed off the bare walls.

Paul had been following me around the place without saying a word. Now he asked, "What is so funny?"

"Look around," I replied. "I think this is Keith's booty barn. There is a plush bed for the dirty deed, a table to allow her a cup of coffee in the morning, and she can tinkle the piano keys while Keith gets her coat out of the closet. He probably tucks a copy of *Winner* into her hopeful hands before hustling her out to the limousine. Then he goes to see his real girlfriend."

"Boy, talk about jumping to conclusions," Paul chuckled. "Actually, this place is a tax write-off for Keith. When you've got that much money, it's hard to find ways to shield it from the IRS."

After we explored the brownstone, Paul sat down at the kitchen table and lapsed into silence once more. Was he worried that I'd jump bail and he'd lose his home?

I decided to check my home voicemail. There were thirty-two messages on my home phone but aside from Alyssa, Pam Silberstein, and Elaine, not one of them was from anyone I knew. Every one of the major talk shows, magazines, newspapers, and wire services had telephoned, seeking an interview and offering staggering amounts of money.

I went back downstairs to the kitchen. Paul was still sitting and staring into space.

"I need to buy something new to wear," I told him. "Will you walk out with me?"

He got up without saying a word and we went back out into the street.

Greenwich Village used to be a community of writers, musicians, painters, and other creative types. Now it was home to young, white, corporate professionals—the high cost of rent had driven the artists over the bridge into Brooklyn.

This neighborhood still had a little charm left. It was full of nooks, crannies, side streets, coffeehouses, clothing boutiques, and several places that sold vintage albums and used books that I made a mental note to explore when things settled down a little.

After walking five blocks, we found a supermarket and a cheap clothing outlet. I bought a toothbrush, toothpaste, bread, bacon, cheese, crackers, eggs, orange juice, a pack of panties, a new sweat suit, and a pair of pajamas.

As we carried my packages back up the steps, I remembered something.

"Paul, I have a little chore to take care of and I think you should stay outside so you can truthfully say later that you don't know anything about it."

"Jackie, I'm sorry I left you alone for so long to deal with all this, but I'm here now and I'm not going anywhere until this is all over. What is it that you're going to do?"

I told him how anxious Detective Gilchrist was to get his hands on my Filofax the night I was arrested. He had probably cursed that poor rookie cop out by now for allowing it back into my hands. That meant he was going to serve me with a subpoena to get it back. The organizer had to go.

My hands shook as I turned the keys. I locked the door carefully behind us and searched the kitchen drawers until I found a box of matches.

As Paul watched nervously, I burned every single page of my Filofax and watched all the negative comments I had made about Annabelle and Craig, along with my obsessive scribblings about Victor, go swirling down the toilet.

I leaned on the sink and cried.

"Jackie, you're exhausted. Why don't you clean yourself up and take a nap. I'm going to the office and handle some stuff but I'll be back later, okay?"

After Paul left, I bathed and washed my hair with soap. Then I climbed into Keith's bed and went to sleep.

The phone woke me up. I looked at my watch. It was five o'clock! I had slept the whole day away!

There was a pretty French phone, white with pink roses swirling around it, on Keith's nightstand. I lifted the receiver. "Hello?"

It was Mama. "Are you all right?" I asked.

"I'm fine, honey." She sounded like her old sprightly self. What was going on?

"Well, you certainly sound happy."

"Me and Elvira are gonna be on TV tonight. I made them reporters wait right in the living room while I put on my good black dress. I used some of the makeup you left here. Is that all right?"

"Mama, I don't care about the makeup. Why didn't you talk to them on the street?"

"It was Keith's idea to let 'em in. I showed them your baby pictures, the awards you got for spelling in elementary school, and your college diploma."

Oh, Mother of God.

"Mama, is Keith still there? I need to talk to him."

"He left a few minutes ago . . . said he was going to see you. Jackie, he is such a nice man. Don't let him get away, okay?"

This was surreal. Here I was getting closer and closer to the electric chair and Mama was still trying to get me married. "Mama, I am not thinking about Keith in any kind of romantic way. All I want him to do is get me out of this mess as soon as possible."

"A woman can do both, can't she?"

"Mama, please tell me you didn't give Keith the impression that I'm interested in him."

"Don't you think he is handsome?"

"Of course, but that isn't the point. Will you answer my question?"

"Calm down baby, you getting' all upset for nuthin'. No, I did not tell Keith you're interested in him. A lady never shows her cards first."

I heard a snicker in the background.

"Who is that?"

"Elvira."

"Who else is there?"

"Nobody. Keith chased them all out of here before he left. Me and him got along real good."

"I'm glad, Mama." No matter what she had said or done, it was good to hear her sounding happy again.

"I think he likes you, Jackie."

"Please stop."

"All right, but he promised me that you ain't going

back to jail. He said it the way a man talks about a woman he's interested in."

Keith was just keeping a worried mother from giving in to despair, but why should I burst her bubble? She was going to need all the confidence she had now and a whole lot more before this was over.

"Sure, Mama," I said gently.

"Is Paul still there with you? What kind of place you stayin' in? When can I come see you?"

The questions stumbled over themselves.

"Paul left but he is coming back. I'll ask Keith about you coming here and call you in the morning."

"All right. I love you, baby."

"I love you, too, Mama."

There wasn't anything else to do, so I curled up with a copy of Keith's life story.

Keith Williams was born the youngest of two children to Otis and Eleanor Williams on December 29, 1952, in Buffalo, New York. His father, a plumber, died of a heart attack when Keith was ten and his mother went to work as a cafeteria cook at the local high school. Keith's sister, Dolores, was sixteen at the time. She started babysitting, Keith got a paper route, and the family managed to survive. Dolores disliked school from day one but Keith loved it. Since it was clear that Keith was a scholar and a leader, the two females doted on his every whim. He was the bravest, smartest, best-looking boy in the whole world as far as they were concerned. He felt like the world was his for the taking, and failure never entered his mind.

The only blot in his perfect teenaged life was the fact that at the age of sixteen, he had gone joyriding in a stolen car to prove his manhood to the other boys. "I didn't get caught but for a long time I was scared that the police were going to come banging on our door," he said.

He was valedictorian and voted most likely to succeed in his high school class, and then it was off to Howard University as a scholarship student. He majored in American history. As an undergraduate, Keith noticed that the law and medical students were stars in the girls' eyes on campus. He decided to go to Howard Law School and picked criminal law because of injustice in the system.

After graduation, he spent five years with one firm. He became their brightest and most publicized attorney. He started his own firm and his star never stopped rising.

I did some quick calculations. If he was born in 1952, that meant he had just passed his forty-fifth birthday.

According to the book jacket, Keith owned a home in the Hamptons. There was no mention of the brownstone that was my hiding place.

I, on the other hand, was homeless and scared. Why did some people lead effortlessly charmed lives while others sank slowly no matter how hard they tried to stay afloat?

Throughout the book, it was clear that Keith felt more of an emotional attachment to his sister than he did to his mother. He wanted to marry someday and have children and said, "The woman I marry must be smart, beautiful, passionate about her people, and committed to building her own business and earning her own money."

I had to snort at that. This combination of Coretta Scott King, Dorothy Dandridge, and Berry Gordy-in-a-skirt did not exist, which meant that deep down inside, he didn't really want to get married at all.

I kept on reading, wondering how long I was supposed to stay hidden inside this beautiful dungeon before someone came to check on me.

I was just beginning a section about the trial that made him famous, when I heard noise. I dropped *Winner* and flew down the stairs. Keith and his driver were huffing and puffing through the front door, pushing boxes in front of them.

"What's all this?" I asked.

"The police were finished when I went to check on your apartment. I thought you might like a few of your things," Keith replied. "Somehow I ended up packing up almost every item in your apartment. There are three more boxes in the car. Tell Paul to get down here and help me."

I hugged him gratefully. A gal needs her ornaments and knickknacks before she can settle down.

"Paul went to work. He's coming back later."

"Well, everything is here except the furniture," he laughed. "By the way, I couldn't find any computer disks. Since you're in the writing business, I thought that was kind of strange." He cocked his head to the side and waited for me to answer.

"I have lots of disks. They are all on the computer hutch in a couple of organizers. Right above my laptop computer. Did you bring that?"

"The police must have them," Keith replied.

"Oh, no!" I plunked myself down on the bottom step. I just couldn't take any more.

"Is there anything incriminating on the hard drive or the disks?" Keith asked.

How many disks had I lost? At least two dozen. My whole publishing career, the work of many aspiring writers, partial screenplays that I'd started trying my hand at, plus all my personal correspondence. Worse, the hard drive on my computer would lead them straight into the swirl of obsessive e-mails that I had sent to Victor over the past year.

I wasn't in any mood to talk about that.

"Never mind," he said. "We'll talk about the case to-morrow."

Keith and his driver went out and came back in twice as I sat there feeling like I had been stripped naked.

Finally, they were done and seven boxes sat in the

middle of Keith's polished wood living room floor. "Well, that's everything," he said.

"Did they take my paper files, too?"

"Yes, there wasn't a slip of paper in that apartment." Keith sat down beside me. "Have you eaten today?"

"Just some cheese and crackers."

"There are some nice restaurants a few blocks from here."

"I'm not really hungry, but maybe Paul and I will go out somewhere when he gets back."

He stood up. "Paul is in your corner, Jackie."

"I know."

He ruffled my hair and smiled. "I'll see you tomorrow morning."

Paul brought several cartons of Chinese food with him—fried rice, moo goo gai pan, orange chicken, lo mein, egg rolls, plus bottled water and cans of soda—it all arrived just in time for the six o'clock news. Since the only television was in the upstairs bedroom, we carried everything up there and made small talk while I laid everything out, using the dresser as a serving table. We piled our plates high and sat on separate sides of the bed to eat. The food was fresh and tasty, but it started going down like lumps of clay after Paul found the remote and switched on the TV set.

The story of my arrest and upcoming trial was the lead on all the newscasts. I couldn't believe it. Surely there was something far more newsworthy to report on—weren't there people at war or starving somewhere on the globe?

My mug shot peered back at us from the screen. The media-created biography—Hell's Kitchen girl escapes her background and becomes a publishing executive only to fall back into the gutter from whence she'd come—was repeated with such regularity that I knew if I didn't stop watching, I'd begin to accept it as truth.

I was about to turn it off when Mama and Elvira appeared on the screen.

They looked good. Mama was wearing a square-necked, long-sleeved black dress which she saved for special occasions. A string of pearls that I had given her last Christmas was around her neck and the matching earrings in her ears. She was too vain to appear in public in her natural gray hair so she wore a black wig. Elvira's beige suit hung on her thin frame. She wasn't wearing any jewelry but her short gray hair was brushed to the side. Mama had shared my makeup with her. They both looked very dignified.

The evolution of Jacqueline Naomi Blue unfolded. Mama talked about what a wonderful child I had been— "she never gave me a lick of trouble"—how we didn't have much money but she made sure I always looked nice—"when I didn't have money for new shoes, I slicked up her old ones with Vaseline and made 'em shine"—the way I studied hard and made good grades—"her teachers loved her." The reporter cut to still photos of me as a baby, toddler, girl, and young woman the whole time Mama was talking.

Finally, the conversation turned to Annabelle's death.

"Why do you think your daughter has been charged with murder?"

"She was just in the wrong place at the wrong time."

"Do you think that race plays a part in all this?"

Mama paused. "Probably does, but money got somethin' to do with all this, too. They wouldn't have rushed Jackie into jail so fast if she was rich."

"But your daughter has the best criminal defense attorney that money can buy."

Elvira jumped in, with a look of righteous indignation on her face. "Keith Williams is working for free. If he wasn't in this case, that poor girl would be so far under a jailhouse right now, nobody would ever get her out. What y'all need to do is leave her alone and find out who the real killer is."

Mama had the last word. She held up my second grade school picture (the one with my two front teeth missing) and spoke directly into the camera. "Jackie is not a criminal. If anybody out there knows anything that can help her, please call Keith Williams right now." It was over and as I clicked off the TV, it occurred to me that Mama and Elvira looked younger and had a lot more energy than I'd ever thought to see in them again. My troubles had given them some excitement and a reason to live.

Paul rubbed his forehead. "This is all so unbelievable."

I had lost my appetite a long time ago. Now I sprawled flat on my back across the bed. "I don't know how much more of it I can stand."

"I'm sorry all this is happening to you, Jackie. Unfortunately, it's going to get a whole lot worse before it gets better."

"I know."

He lay down beside me and took my hand. "Don't worry, I'm here for you."

I put my head on his chest. "Paul, you're such a good friend. I still can't believe you've risked your home to set me free."

He took a deep breath. "Jackie, I didn't put my house up because we're friends. I did it because I'm in love with you."

So, that was the reason he'd been silent all day. He was building up the courage to say what he'd been feeling for the past few years.

"Paul, I . . ."

"No. I've got to get this out. I'm tired of walking around pretending to be the good, loyal buddy." He took a deep breath. "Here it is, plain and simple, baby—I want to be your man."

I hugged him around the waist and then looked up to meet his eyes. "Paul, I can't let you make that kind of promise to me right now. I may be going to prison."

Paul caressed my face. "Do you think I don't know that? I love you in spite of this terrible mess, but I need to know how you feel about me."

"I love you, too, but . . ."

I was about to add that I didn't have the kind of heat for him that makes a woman think about a man day and night. His feelings for me were a lot stronger than mine were for him. Before I could say all that, he placed his finger over my lips.

"Ssshhh. That's all I needed to hear." He pressed my body close to his and our lips met. Then our tongues. It turned into a strong and leisurely kiss. We helped each other out of our clothes and he gently ran his hands and lips over my face, breasts, and thighs. "You are the most beautiful lady I've ever seen."

My heart beat fast. My fingers, as I wrapped them around his thick, solid manhood, trembled slightly.

Paul took his time with my nipples. He played with each one gently . . . sucking and nibbling until I was soaking wet and begging for him to fulfill me.

And then it was on.

His ride started out slow, then it escalated until my nails were digging into his strong back before he shifted into a deliberate, steady stroke that made silent tears of pleasure course down my cheeks.

"Are you my woman?" he whispered.

"Yes, Paul."

We moaned, flowed, and created our own dance that tore down the last walls of our platonic friendship.

26

REASONABLE DOUBT

Paul shook me awake. My eyes opened to find him fully dressed and smiling down at me.

"I have to get going, baby," he said.

"What time is it?"

"Just a little before six."

Why are you leaving for work so early?"

He sat down and stroked my naked back. "I need to go home and change clothes. Plus I have to pack some of my things so I don't have to run to Brooklyn every other day." He groaned. "Jackie, I . . . uh . . . never mind."

There was something deep going on. I could smell it. "What's the matter?"

"I have something to do right after work but I'll get here as soon as I can. Will you be okay here alone?"

"Yes, I'll be fine. I don't want you to move in, Paul. We need time to adjust to our relationship and trying to live together right now would be way too much."

"But your life could be in danger," he protested.

I sat up and stretched. "Paul, let's take this thing slowly, okay?"

He raised his hands in surrender. "Fine. What are your plans for the day?"

"Keith will be here at nine to discuss the case and then I have an important phone call to make. After that, I'm going to see Mama, if he'll allow it."

Paul stood up and glanced at his watch. "Okay, but keep in touch and let me know what's going on. I'll get back here this evening as quickly as possible."

His forehead creased into a frown and there was a sudden emotion in his eyes that I couldn't read.

"Paul, where are you going after work?"

He kissed me on the lips. "There is something I have to take care of, but nothing for you to worry about. Now, get up and come lock up after me."

I couldn't go back to sleep, so six in the morning found me unpacking boxes and hanging my suits, dresses, pants, and blouses in Keith's bedroom closet, which only contained empty hangers. My shoes and boots lined up nicely on the floor of it with plenty of room to spare. It found me packing away my nightgowns, panties, bras, slips, jeans, and sweaters in the nine drawers of a beautiful white, mirror-topped dresser that faced the king-sized bed. Perfume, makeup, nail polish, jewelry box, and the manicure set now dwelled on the top of the dresser. My CD player and two dozen CDs went on the floor beside the bed because there was no other surface to place them on. I left the boxes of books downstairs on the living room floor.

Since the bedroom and kitchen were the only furnished rooms in the entire house, I didn't have a lot of options.

Where should I put the giant piggy bank? Videotapes? Teddy bear? Hair scrunchies? Board games? Top shelf of the closet! The blow dryer and curling iron went up there, too, and it was over.

Keith showed up shortly after nine with orange juice and donuts.

We set up shop at the kitchen table. The crisp morning daylight streamed in through the bay windows and illuminated our tense faces. I was supposed to be at my desk right now, taking calls from agents and writers. When I looked at Keith, eating breakfast and secure in his job, it made me angry and scared. What kind of work would I find when this was all over?

I fastened my gaze on him. "Well, has your detective turned up anything useful?"

Even though my tone was nasty, Keith's expression did not change when he answered. "There have been some revelations."

"Like?"

"Joe Long doesn't like you."

My brain struggled to seize and accept the notion as Keith licked jelly from the inside of a donut—his features unreadable.

I finally managed to squeak out a meek-sounding "Why not?"

He wiped his hands on a napkin. "I was hoping you could tell me."

"I don't have any idea."

"Jealousy, perhaps?"

"I can't think of any reason for Joe to be jealous of me. We were both senior editors at our firms. I may have earned a little more than he does, but not enough for him to hate me for it."

"Did you have more power than he does?"

I had to snicker. "Everyone in the Black Pack has more power than Joe does. Why is he singling me out for his bitterness?"

I had spoken the truth. Joe was simply Black window dressing at the place where he worked and his opinion didn't count for much.

Keith checked his notes. "Would you describe Joe Long as a mentally stable person?"

"Yes. I've only seen him get angry once in the five years I've known him. Why do you ask?"

He ignored my question. "Tell me about it."

I told him about the night Dallas told us that Victor had been coming out of Victoria's Secret and might have made a new "love connection."

"Joe went nuts," I concluded. "Maybe they were both in love with the same woman or something."

"I'll have one of my private investigators look into it."

"Why is that important?"

Keith said, "Right now, everything is important."

"Dallas also told me that she thinks Joe is a closet homosexual with a crush on Victor. Have you heard anything like that?"

"I'm not willing to say right now, Jackie."

"Fine. What else?"

"Annabelle was having an affair," said Keith.

For some reason, I wasn't surprised. "Who is the other man?"

"That's what we don't know yet," Keith said with a frown. "Apparently it's been going on for quite some time. Her friends know that the man exists but she never revealed his identity. "Have you seen this bullshit?" He waved a copy of *Time* magazine in my face. "According to these folks, Annabelle Welburn Murray was an alabaster saint. Not a woman who paid her household help worse than anyone else at The Dakota, and was fucking around on her husband."

"Do you think the other man killed her?"

Keith's eyes met mine. "Not unless he was already in that apartment when you stopped by for the book. Is there any chance of that?"

"She had been crying, so it is possible."

He was staring at me.

"What is it?" I was not in the mood for any more puzzles.

"I've reviewed all the videotape for that morning, starting at five A.M. If her lover was in the apartment, then he had to live in her building. Every other man who came in or out has been accounted for. Unfortunately, I cannot subpoena every single male who lives in that building without cause."

"What about Craig? Have you ruled him out?"

"Craig Murray was faithful to this Jezebel and there is absolutely no way he could have killed her, either."

"Are you sure?"

"Positive. I have accounted for every single second of his time during the crucial period."

"Where was he?"

"At his sister's home. He and Annabelle had a fight and he left, taking the kid with him."

"Break it down for me, Keith. What does this mean?"

"It means that I've never had a case with more holes in it than this one." Keith was clearly delighted. "It has 'reasonable doubt' written all over it. Jackie, you're gonna walk. Take my word for it."

"In other words, you may not find out who killed her."

"Exactly."

"I cannot live my life under a cloud of suspicion, Keith."

"My people will keep trying, but I just wanted you to know that it may not be possible." He patted my arm. "Let's talk about the computer and disks that the police took away. "Is there anything incriminating on those disks or the hard drive?"

It was time to tell him the story of Victor Bell.

". . . uh . . . um . . ."

"Jackie, you can't let me get blindsided in that courtroom. I've got to know."

My hands flew up to cover my face. "It's all just so embarrassing."

"Not half as unsettling as what goes on in a women's prison."

Damn, he was blunt!

I hung my head in shame and stared down at the kitchen table and never took my eyes off its wooden surface as I poured out my pathetic saga of lust, obsession, and humiliation.

When I got to the part where Paul fled down the stairs after seeing me in my slip, Keith made a noise that sounded suspiciously like a choked-back snicker.

He sucked in his breath when I described the sound of Victor retching in my bathroom.

"That's it," I said finally.

He tapped his pen on the table and it was clear he was thinking out loud. "I've been told that Victor and Joe Long are good friends. Is that true?"

"Yes, but I can tell you right now that no one in the Black Pack had a reason to kill Annabelle."

"You're probably right, but I'm going to have a talk with Victor anyway."

"About what?"

He neatly sidestepped the question. "Maybe I just want to get a real good look at this brother. I'm wondering what he has that would make a smart, good-looking woman like you go to such lengths to get him."

I rolled my eyes toward the ceiling as though Keith was full of shit, but he was making me feel good inside.

"I also want to look into the eyes of a man who had you alone and willing in a bedroom and ran out. I can't imagine what such a fool would look like."

He winked at me and I smiled back at him.

"Perhaps," Keith continued, "the poor man needs to be in a hospital for the criminally insane. I can arrange that, you know."

Victor in a straitjacket! The image struck me as funny and I got a bad case of the giggles. Soon Keith was laughing, too.

I chose a vanilla-frosted donut and poured myself some juice.

"Let's talk about little Dora Murray."

"Did you find out what was wrong with her?" I asked.

"There was nothing wrong with the child."

"But she said that the doctor gave her a needle."

"The doctor wasn't putting medicine into her body," Keith replied. "He was taking blood out."

"Why?"

Keith grinned. "For DNA testing."

I jumped up and started waving my arms around like I'd just won a race. "I knew that child wasn't Craig's. Both her parents are blond but she looks Hispanic. Have you seen her yet?"

He waited until I had calmed down. "No, but that can wait."

I slumped back into my seat.

"Poor Craig. This is awful. Is there any way to keep Craig from finding out about this DNA business? He adores that kid."

Keith leaned forward. "Jackie, I need you to understand something. Look at me."

I looked.

"I'm going to find out what those test results are and when we walk into that courtroom, the gloves are off. There is nothing I won't do, no reputation that will go untarnished, no secret unrevealed, in my effort to win. I intend to get a 'not guilty' verdict in this case."

I said nothing.

Keith cleared his throat. "All right, let's start making a list of people to call as character witnesses. Folks who will say under oath that you are the greatest thing since sliced bread and couldn't kill a fly."

"Well, forget Joe," I said bitterly. "What about the rest of the group?"

"Rachel, Alyssa, and Paul are totally on your side. I'm not sure about Victor yet."

"Rachel?" I couldn't have been more astonished if he had said Batman.

"Yeah. She is really pissed off about what has happened to you and blames Tiffany Nixon and her column for pushing this thing forward so fast."

"Are we talking about Rachel Edwards from the Black Pack?"

Keith seemed amused. "Yes. Why are you so surprised?"

"Because Rachel only cares about getting a rich husband."

"You're very wrong about her," Keith said softly. "Besides, I don't just want a list of publishing folks." He pushed some paper and a pen in my direction. "Write down the names of everyone you have a good relationship with. Neighbors, your local dry cleaner . . . don't leave anyone out."

After Keith left, I called Elaine Garner. Even though she had not put up my bail, I still wanted to do the book. The money would go to Mama, who had been pinching pennies all her life. Elaine didn't want to talk on the phone but agreed to come over for a long lunch. I warned her not to tell anyone about my location. The last thing I needed was a horde of reporters camped outside the brownstone.

Elaine drank Bailey's over ice. I'd have to find a liquor store and then stop by the supermarket to pick up some kind of finger food.

She arrived promptly at noon with a basket of fruit and a bouquet of flowers. "Jackie, it is such a relief to see you in person."

I took the gifts and her coat and spoke over my

shoulder as I went in search of a hanger and a vase. "I don't know how to thank you, Elaine."

When I came back she was thumbing through a copy of *Winner.* There was a smile on her face. "This is a big fish, Jackie. I hope you're trying to reel him in."

"Not at all," I replied crisply. "I have far more important things on my mind."

She put the book down. "I'm not saying he should be the only item on your 'Things to Do' list, but he should definitely be in one of the top three slots."

I had to laugh at that. "Come on. We have to sit in the kitchen."

"Why isn't there any furniture in the living room?"

I told her about the upstairs bedroom and my idea about Keith's way of handling one-night stands as I bustled about the kitchen, fixing drinks and putting food on the table.

Elaine got a kick out of my theory. "Imagine being rich enough to indulge those kind of whims," she sighed.

I sat down and we sipped our alcohol quietly for a moment. "Tell me what is going on, Elaine. I'm completely out of the loop."

"Jackie, you are the only topic of conversation when I'm at work—then I watch every bit of the newscast when I'm at home."

"So, what is the verdict?"

She shrugged. "No one really knows what to believe."

I gazed at her intently. "What do you believe, Elaine?"

She took a deep breath. "The motive doesn't work for me or anyone else in the book business, Jackie. Nobody in their right mind would literally kill to become executive editor. This isn't Wall Street! We are the most underpaid people in the world. To be frank, many people think you were having an affair with Craig Murray and things got out of hand."

Elaine was being honest with me, but her response wasn't what I'd expected. She was supposed to say that I was not capable of taking a human life. How could I feel so insecure inside and appear so severe on the outside?

"Well, they're wrong," I said sternly. "Let's talk about our project."

Elaine and I ate buffalo wings, nachos and cheese, chips and dip while we discussed the memoir which would keep Mama financially safe if I went to prison. The book would easily be worth half a million dollars. We decided that Elaine would rent a post office box and I would send daily updates on the case to her there. She would start searching for a superstar crime writer to cover the trial. If I were convicted, New York's Son of Sam law would prevent me from making money, so it would then become my mother's story "as told to" the superstar writer. Elaine would walk Mama through the publishing process until the money was safe in the bank. Although I asked her to report any news she heard on the case back to me, Elaine made it clear that she would not do it.

"I won't become part of the story," she said, "unless I overhear the real killer confess to the crime."

In the end, we handwrote an agreement that I would not take the project to another editor.

I kissed her cheek at the door.

She winked at me and walked out.

I had forgotten to ask Keith about going to see my mama but I needed to do it, no matter how many reporters were perched on her stoop. There was no one outside when the cab pulled up in front of her building—perhaps the interview she'd given was enough to feed them for a while.

She hugged me like I'd just been released from Leavenworth before snatching Elaine's fruit basket from my hand. "Oh, Jackie, you spent too much money!"

I hung my coat up in the living room closet, "No, I didn't. A friend of mine gave it to me."

Mama placed the basket on her kitchen countertop and ripped the plastic covering off it. "Look at this! My, ain't this somethin'," she crowed.

"I brought you some money, too. It should be time to fill your prescriptions again, right?"

She hesitated in a way I didn't like. "Jackie, you can't afford to do that anymore. I'll be okay."

"Don't be silly," I said. "Do you have anything cold to drink? I'm thirsty." I opened the refrigerator and there was only a jar of mayonnaise, two leftover pork chops, and a dozen eggs.

"I haven't had time to go shopping," she said.

It was amazing how the events of the last few weeks had changed me. I could smell the lie as it came out of her mouth. "I don't believe you."

She took an apple from the basket and bit it. "Girl, I know you done lost your mind. How you gonna stand there and call your own mother a liar?"

"Mama, I have never seen you eat a piece of fruit without washing it first. You're hungry, and I want to know why."

"If I'm hungry, it's because that Weight Watchers group I'm in is real strict."

"Really?" I placed my hands on my hips. "I'm going across the hall right now and talk to Elvira about this group."

"No!"

"Why not?"

She said nothing, so I marched to the door.

"Please don't."

My hand was on the knob. "Why? Because you've never been to Weight Watchers and Elvira won't know what I'm talking about, will she?"

The apple went down on the counter. "No."

Then Mama was slumped on the sofa, crying into her hands. I sat bewildered, with one arm around her thin shoulders. "What is it, Mama? Is there some gang in the building taking your money?"

She shook her head and took a deep breath to get control of herself. "There ain't no gang, baby. My medicine started goin' up months ago. I tried takin' it every other day, but then I didn't feel good so I went to half a pill every day and things got worse. So now I buy what I'm supposed to buy and there just ain't no money left over to buy a lot of food."

This was truly baffling. I paid Mama's rent, utilities, and gave her $200 a month for food and medicine. "What are you talking about?"

"Come here." She took me by the hand and led me into the bedroom. She kept her prescription bottles in a nightstand drawer. "This," she said, holding up one slim bottle, "is Vasotec for my high blood pressure . . . thirty pills cost $100." She picked up a fat vial. "This is Ultracet that I gotta take for arthritis . . . ninety pills cost $150 now."

There was one last container. A fat bottle of green pills called Cardizem CD. "How much are these?"

"Those are for my arthritis, too. They cost $135 for only sixty pills."

"Mama, why didn't you tell me that what I give you isn't nearly enough?"

She shook her head sadly. "It ain't your fault that I left school. You shouldn't have to take care of me. I don't know what to do anymore, Jackie."

I grabbed her by the shoulders, sat her down on the bed, and knelt on the floor beside her.

"Mama, I'm going to tell you something but you can't even tell Elvira. If you do, I'm going to get in a lot of trouble with Keith and that won't be good at all."

"I won't say nuthin,' but what's goin' on now, Jackie?"

I rubbed her hands. "Mama, no matter how things

turn out with my trial, you and I are going to come into a lot of money. At least half a million dollars."

Her eyes got wide as saucers and she drew her hands back like my own were burning hot. She looked suspicious and disappointed all at the same time. "Jackie, you swore to me that you didn't have nuthin' to do with what happened to that poor woman. What in the world have you done?"

It would have been funny if the whole situation weren't just so damned desperate and tragic. "Mama, I did not kill Annabelle and this is not her money. This is money that as far as I'm concerned, I've already earned. My reputation is tarnished, to say the least, I've been arrested and thrown into exile, and still have a trial to get through." The anger was building inside of me and my tone became strident. "I should get a billion dollars for pain and suffering when this is all over, but I won't. The best I'm able to do for myself is sell the inside story of my ordeal."

I told her about my deal with Elaine. "So get up, put your clothes on, and let's go shopping for food, medicine, and whatever else you've been doing without."

She looked doubtful.

By now I was shouting at her. "Look, I know you didn't want to worry me or ask for more, but this is ridiculous. I was bringing home $50,000 a year after taxes and giving you another $200 a month would not have been a struggle."

"Stop hollering at me, Jackie. You buy fancy clothes. Your rent is $2,000 a month, and every time I talk to you, it seems like you just been to some fancy restaurant. You and your Black Pack, just eatin' and drinkin' like y'all the first folks to ever be Black with problems. It's all stupid, but that's your life. Who was I to stop you from eatin' and talkin' 'bout bein' Black? I jus' took what you gave me and stretched it like I always done."

By now she was standing up, her eyes were on fire, and I understood on a very deep level that compared to the problems of her generation, those of the Black Pack seemed inconsequential.

Deflated, I slumped into the armchair. "Fine. I have $10,000 in my bank account. There is no reason for you to jeopardize your health or go hungry. So, let's go shopping."

She wasn't through. "So, you got $10,000 in the bank. That means you got five months' rent for a place you can't even stay in, Jackie. And how long is that gonna last?"

"I don't know, Mama."

"Well, girl, you better start knowin'. This thing you and Elaine got goin' might work but it might not. You need to get rid of that apartment because that $10,000 is all you can count on. Ask Keith to let you put the furniture in the place where you stayin' and then you won't have to pay storage."

"Is that it?"

She smiled and kissed me on the cheek. "No, that ain't it, baby. Tell Keith that the next time some reporters wants to talk to you or me, they better have their checkbooks with 'em because we need the money."

27

CHOCOLATE-COVERED STRAWBERRIES

My plan for getting even with Miss Tiffany Nixon was coming together but it was so bodacious that every time I thought about it, my courage waned a little more. So, there was nothing left to do for the rest of the day except go back to the brownstone.

I took a cab back down to Greenwich Village, feeling exhausted from the heated exchange I'd had with Mama a few hours before. It also saddened me deeply to know that I'd have to give up my own apartment, but it was the only sensible thing to do.

I sprawled out on the living room floor, listening to an old Whitney Houston song called *You Give Good Love*. The pain-filled lyrics enveloped the room, a fitting accompaniment to my own despair. The doorbell rang just as I was contemplating suicide.

"Who is it?"

"Paul."

I unlocked the door and was about to throw my arms around his waist until I saw his face. There were scratch marks on each cheek and his right eye was reddened and beginning to swell.

I was horrified. "Who did this to you?"

Paul closed the door behind him and held me tightly in his arms. His voice was raw with emotion. "I went to Rosa's house that night after I caught you waiting for Victor. We ended up in bed and after that . . . well, we were pretty much a couple. Then you called. My first instinct was to hang up but I couldn't."

"Nothing happened between me and Victor that night. We did not have sex, okay?"

He sighed. "Thank you for letting me know that, baby. Anyway, I didn't tell her that I was putting up my house for your bail or that I was going to tell you how I felt. When you and I finally got it together last night, I felt I owed her an explanation and telling her the truth by phone felt cowardly."

"Did Rosa do this to you?" I touched his eye and he winced.

"Yes. I went to see her this evening to tell her that we're through. She didn't handle it well at all."

I kissed him on the lips and squeezed him hard. "I'm sorry."

"I deserved what I got. It was wrong of me to use her just because you were interested in someone else."

So Paul had bedded Rosa and then kicked her to the curb. Yes, he'd earned the punch and scratches, but I was still angry at her for hurting him.

He allowed me to put a cold compress on his eye as we relaxed on the bed upstairs. I told him about needing to give up the apartment and move my furniture into the brownstone.

"Damn, honey. I'm so sorry."

The rest of my day spilled out. "My mother has been starving herself halfway to death because she can't afford the high cost of medicine and the rent on my apartment is $2,000 per month plus utilities and cable.

It won't take me long to run through $10,000, which is all I have in the bank."

"Hey, Jackie," his tone was softer. "It's gonna be okay. Keith and I will handle everything. We'll have you out of the lease and your furniture in place by Saturday. Now, let's talk about the case. Who do you think did this thing?"

I bit my lip. "Keith isn't sharing much with me. But if you look at it logically, the only person who had both means and opportunity is Annabelle's sister."

"What about motive?"

"That's what I have to find out."

Paul sat up suddenly. "What does that mean?

"It means I can't just sit in this house and do nothing."

He took my chin in his hand. "Jackie, what are you planning to do?"

"I'll tell you about it over dinner. Let's find a good restaurant—I'm hungry."

He motioned toward his eye. "This hurts. How about an indoor picnic?"

I gave him a half-smile. "I don't feel like cooking."

"Me, either." He checked his watch. "Why don't I go pick up some champagne, okay? What kind do you want?"

"Dom Perignon."

"Damn. Who is paying for all this?"

"Keith. He told me to get whatever I want."

"Okay. What about Cristal?"

I made a face. "Dom Perignon tastes better."

"Fine. What would you like for dinner?"

"Lobster, shrimp, and caviar."

Paul laughed. "When Keith gets this bill, he's going to take back what he said, so we might as well enjoy his generosity for the night. Would you like me to rent some videos?"

"If you want."

"Okay. Put on something pretty and I'll be back in an hour."

"What about dessert?"

I could tell by the look on his face that he wanted to say something naughty but then he collected himself. "We're going to have chocolate-covered strawberries," he declared smoothly.

When the door closed behind him, I turned Whitney off and took a hot bath, which soothed my frazzled nerves.

What to wear? What to wear for our romantic indoor picnic? I hunted around in the closet and came up with a sleeveless, clingy, yellow dress that hung down to my ankles.

Paul loved it. He pressed me close to him, and as we kissed, I could feel his erection growing. I pushed him away. "Later, baby, I'm really starving."

He took a quick shower as I unpacked the delicacies and came out wearing a pair of blue silk pajamas. We sat cross-legged in front of the food, which was laid out on a pretty white comforter, and started filling our paper plates.

"Paul, where does Keith live?"

"He has an apartment in the residential section of Trump Tower and a home up in Connecticut. Why do you ask?"

"Just curious. He just appears and disappears without saying very much about himself."

"Did you read *Winner?*"

"Yeah. It's not like I couldn't find a copy."

He laughed. "What do you think of it?"

"It's very good. Where is his family now?"

"Keith's mother lives in Houston, which is where she is originally from. Dolores lives in Scarsdale with her husband and fourteen-year-old son. Her husband works for Keith as an administrator."

"Oh. Does he fly down to Houston a lot?"

"He sees his mother four or five times a year."

"There is some sort of tension between Keith and his mother. The book leaves a lot of questions unanswered."

He paused while loading shrimp onto his plate. "That's what I told him while we were working on it. He wanted to encourage college students to enter law school and didn't want to delve too much into his personal life. What is it that you want to know?"

I shrugged nonchalantly. "Why is he still single?"

"His college sweetheart wanted to get hitched during the summer between college and law school but Keith got cold feet at the last minute. He came close to getting married again right after the Buchanan case ended. He was seeing one woman exclusively for two years and was thinking about popping the question when she started putting the pressure on him. It became unbearable and when she gave the ultimatum, they broke up."

"Two years! He was dating her for two whole years and didn't marry her?"

He started eating. "I would do the same thing to you but we're too old. I want at least five kids and there isn't much time."

"Five kids! Are you out of your mind? You'll be too old to even pick up the last baby," I laughed.

He pretended to be insulted as he flexed one arm. "I don't know what you're talking about. Look at the shape I'm in."

I waved away his flexing arm. "What movies did you rent?"

"Not so fast. You promised to tell me about this detective work you're planning."

Slowly and carefully I laid out my plan.

Paul listened until I was done. "Jackie, what if there are no skeletons in Tiffany Nixon's closet?"

"Then I'll find another reporter who has one."

"I didn't know you could be so devious. To be honest, it's a little scary."

Tears sprang to my eyes. "Then find a woman who isn't facing life in prison. She'll be the person I was before that cell door slammed on me."

His arms were around me in an instant. "Hey there, girl. Take it easy. You're the only woman for me, and I'll help you with this plan, even though I think it is far too risky. Right now, Tiffany Nixon is just trying to sell papers. If she gets angry on a personal level, she could make things rough for you and really damage Keith's reputation."

"It's a chance I'm going to take. An acquittal just isn't good enough for me, Paul. I want Annabelle's sister behind bars and my own name cleared."

"Fine. There's a lot of hard work ahead of us, but let's just try to relax tonight." He gestured toward the bag at his feet. "I picked up *She's Gotta Have It*, *School Daze*, *Do the Right Thing*, and *Jungle Fever*. We'll have our own Spike Lee Film Festival, okay?"

"Paul, that's eight hours' worth of movies!"

"Do you mean to tell me that a young woman like you can't stay up all night?"

"Nope! I'm not that young anymore. So pick one."

He laughed.

"Hey, wait a minute! What kind of Spike Lee Film Festival is this? You forgot *Mo' Better Blues* and *Malcolm X!*"

He threw up his hands. "No way. You'll forget that there is a living, breathing man in the room with you. I'm far too smart to even try and compete with Denzel Washington."

That was funny. "So, which one are we watching?"

"I choose *She's Gotta Have It*."

I shook my head and spoke around a mouth full of seafood. "No way. Too sexy. Let's watch *School Daze*."

Paul smiled wryly. "I went to Morehouse, remember? Pick again."

We settled on *Jungle Fever.*

What a wonderful evening! We talked, laughed, ate ourselves silly, drank two bottles of champagne, and got into the movie like neither one of us had ever seen it before. We didn't talk about the case and after a while I didn't feel like a murder suspect.

But that night, my dreams shattered our peace.

My hands were wrapped around Annabelle's slim, white throat. Her silky blond hair was turning red as blood spurted from the top of her head and flowed through it, yet she was still able to scream, "Astrid gets the job—ha ha ha ha ha," in a taunting, singsongy, little-kid voice. I squeezed tighter, and her eyes bugged out but that didn't stop her from shrieking, "All about Moms! All about Moms!" over and over again.

I woke up screaming in the middle of the night. Paul and I wrapped ourselves around each other and talked quietly. We didn't even try to go back to sleep.

28

PAMELA SILBERSTEIN

Paul was as good as his word. Within a week, all the furniture from my old apartment had been moved into the brownstone. The place now felt like home.

Every time I turned around, Jamal Hunt was on television talking about what a raw deal the media was giving me. Of course, he always managed to work the title of his current novel into the conversation. As a result, it hit *The New York Times* bestseller list and stayed there for six weeks.

Keith continued to stonewall me. He refused to tell me everything he had under his fingernails or talk to me about the strategy he would use in the courtroom. He just kept saying that he was satisfied we had more than enough reasonable doubt to win an acquittal.

The only way my own plot could fail was if Tiffany Nixon had never done anything wrong in her entire professional life—how many people can honestly say that?

I needed one of the editors to get me a dossier on Nixon. There was no point in asking Joe, and I'd never really trusted Dallas. It was clear that Nixon's motive had always been to score points among powerful conservative factions in order to advance her career, so she wasn't likely to cozy up with Elaine or Alyssa. I needed a white editor whom I could trust. I needed Pam Silberstein.

It was the first week of May. She agreed to meet me at our old haunt, Café Un Deux Trois on 44th Street. I took the subway uptown and every straphanger who gawked at me received a cold, direct stare in return.

I saw Pam's red hair as soon as I walked into the eatery. She was seated on a stool at the crowded bar. She had saved a seat for me by placing her briefcase on the stool beside her. We exchanged hugs and she put the case in her lap.

"What are you drinking, kiddo?" she asked cheerfully.

"Ginger ale."

"What?"

"I have to keep my head real clear for the next few weeks, Pam."

She nodded soberly. "When does the trial start?"

"In three weeks."

"Are you frightened?"

Was I frightened? Not at that exact moment. My adrenaline was pumping too high and the desire for revenge was too prominent in my mind for fear to sneak its way in. But I couldn't say all this to Pam without scaring her away.

"Yeah, I'm terrified."

She downed the contents of her glass and summoned the bartender. "Another straight Scotch for me and a ginger ale for my friend."

"Pam, I need you to do me a huge favor."

"Is it exciting, illegal, unethical, or immoral?" Her face was creased in a huge grin like a mischievous schoolgirl.

"Unethical," I replied.

The bartender placed a fresh drink in front of her and I let her sip on it for a few minutes. In the meantime, I took stock of the customers around me. There were no other Black people in the room but I was used to that. There were more women than men at the bar and a lot of couples eating in the dining room.

"What is it that you need me to do?"

"Huh?"

"What is the unscrupulous behavior that you want me to engage in?"

I turned my back on the dining room and got back to business. "How would you like to acquire a book by Tiffany Nixon?"

Pam made a face. "What is she writing about and why do you, of all people, want to help her?"

"I'm not trying to help her, Pam."

Silence. Pam was eyeing me impatiently, hoping that I'd get to the point as quickly as possible. I didn't blame her.

"I just wondered if you would approach Nixon about the possibility of doing a book on a subject of her choosing."

"And if she says yes?"

"Then, as an editor, you would not be out of line if you asked her for a resumé, all the biographical information that she has, plus a collection of every story she has ever written."

Pam's mouth was hanging open.

"Then," I continued, "you could make a copy of everything she gives you and pass the copied file on to me. If the two of you meet and a good book idea comes out of it, then please feel free to publish it. I won't have any hard feelings."

Pam's mouth closed.

"If you don't like anything she has to say, simply send her back the material and call it a day. Editors do that all the time—she'll have no reason to be suspicious."

Pam let out a whoosh of air. "What are you going to do with the information?"

"I can't tell you that."

"Why not?"

"Because I don't want to jinx my plan by talking about it."

She suddenly looked worried. "Jackie, I'm your friend but you'll have to give me some time to think about this."

"How much time, Pam?"

"At least a week."

It was far too long, but what could I do?

In the meantime, I turned my thoughts to the possible motive of Sarah Jane Welburn Rizzelli. What would make a woman kill her own sister? Paul said that it was either money or a man.

I was coming out of the drugstore one afternoon, mulling over ways to find out more about Sarah Jane, when I heard someone call my name. When I turned around, a blast of liquid hit me in the face and then a fierce blow landed in my stomach. I fell to the ground, holding my face, with my eyes squeezed tight shut, and screaming.

I heard voices above me:

"Lady, are you all right?"

"Somebody call the police!"

"I saw who did it. It was a female and she ran around the corner."

"Don't move, an ambulance is on the way!"

By the time paramedics arrived, the pain in my stomach had subsided and I realized that the liquid was not acid . . . only lukewarm coffee. I jumped in a cab to get away from the crowd that had gathered.

29

ANNABELLE ON THE DOWN LOW

It was hard to tell who was angrier. Both Keith and Paul were huffing and puffing so hard, they looked like blowfish.

I was lying on the sofa, hoping that the attack on me wouldn't make the papers. It might give my poor mama a heart attack.

"Jackie, did the woman's voice sound familiar?"

"I think so, but I'm really not sure."

"That's very important," Keith asserted. "We need to know whether it was just some nut who recognized you from all the media coverage and threw the coffee at you on impulse, or is there a woman following you around?"

Paul pounded his fist into his palm. "This woman threw coffee in her face and punched her in the stomach. Instead of a fist, it could just as easily have been a knife. What are you going to do to keep her safe, Keith?"

"She can stay in this house and not go out that door for any reason or I can have one of my men take her everywhere she wants to go. The choice is hers."

Paul calmed down. "I like the second idea."

"No," I protested. "That isn't going to work for me."

"Jackie, you could have been killed today," said Paul.

"I don't care. Being followed around all the time would be worse than death. But there is something else at stake here. If this was a random act, it only drives home what I've been saying about the need to clear my name. Otherwise, I'll have to watch my back for the rest of my life."

Keith shook his head. "Jackie, we've been through this before. I have my suspicions about what happened to Annabelle and why, but as of right now, there is still no way for me to prove it."

"You're right. I just needed to hear you say that one more time."

Keith didn't pick up on the warning. Someday he would learn that I had taken matters into my own hands, but he wouldn't be able to say that I did not give him a chance.

"Will you tell me what your suspicions are?"

"Yes, but not now."

My head drooped.

"However, I do have some news about Victor Bell that may interest the two of you."

My eyes widened with curiosity.

Paul glowered. "What is it?"

Keith grinned. "He was having an affair with Annabelle Murray."

"What!" Paul and I screamed in unison.

"I don't believe it," Paul said. "Why would a rich and beautiful woman want to fool around with that creep? In fact, how did she even know he existed?"

"He met her at the Book Expo convention in Chicago a few years ago. They had drinks. They went to her hotel room and had sex. Things must have gone extremely well that night because they continued to see each other quite a bit over the past few years."

Fireworks went off in my head and I sat bolt upright. "Do you think Victor killed her?"

Keith shook his head. "No. He was having breakfast with another member of your Black Pack when Annabelle was killed."

"Joe Long," I guessed.

"Right."

Paul shrugged. "I don't care about all that. I just want you to tell Jackie that she has to have the body-guard."

Keith looked at his watch. "I'll leave you two love-birds to wrestle with the bodyguard issue. In the mean-time, I'm going to try and get my hands on any security video cameras that may be in the area. Maybe we'll get lucky and find a moving image of this woman in action. Grabbing her won't be difficult once we know what she looks like."

We didn't get lucky and I refused to accept a body-guard or stay in the house. As a result, Paul spent more time at my place than he did at his own.

30

PAM'S FOLDER

So Victor liked white girls, which explained why I'd never had a chance. Annabelle was a tramp and had probably been one since the day Craig married her, which was why Dora appeared to be of Mediterranean descent. Keith said none of this shed any light on who Dora's father actually was or if he had anything to do with Annabelle's murder.

I was surfing the Internet looking for information on Tiffany Nixon one morning and wondering if Pam Bernstein would ever contact me again, when her folder arrived by messenger. I forced all thoughts about Victor and his disgusting little life out of my mind to concentrate on the task before me.

On the surface, the thick dossier that Pam provided didn't seem very interesting. Everything was meticulously typed and in chronological order—I would have to investigate each piece of paper line by line and hope to strike paydirt.

Elaine was fascinated by this turn of events. Even though I never used Pam Silberstein's name, I'm sure she figured it out. Pam would become the book's Deep Throat.

There are skeletons in everyone's closet, I told myself, hoping that when the bones tumbled out of Tiffany Nixon's cupboard there would be a Janet Cooke/Jimmy's World carcass somewhere in the debris.

Janet Cooke was once a respected journalist at the *Washington Post*. On September 29, 1980, she published "Jimmy's World," a heartrending tale of a grade school heroin addict. According to Ms. Cooke, Jimmy was "eight years old and a third-generation heroin addict, a precocious little boy with sandy hair, velvety brown eyes, and needle marks freckling the baby-smooth skin of his thin, brown arms." The public was outraged. They wrote and called the *Washington Post*, demanding the boy's immediate rescue from his horrific home life. When Janet declined to give his address, saying that drug dealers would kill her if she did, the government stepped in to search for the tot. Their efforts were fruitless but the story was so well written that on April 13, 1981, Janet was awarded the Pulitzer Prize for investigative reporting. The intense media interest in Janet and Jimmy caused her story to unravel faster than a ball of yarn in a cat's paw. It turned out that there was no Jimmy. She had made the whole thing up. Forced to return the prize and resign in humiliation, Janet became unemployable and was last seen selling women's garments at a department store in the Midwest.

What if I investigated every story that Tiffany Nixon had ever written and found something close to a Jimmy? And what if I used that information to gain her cooperation—I could feed her information that would make Annabelle's killer panic and make a mistake.

Unbelievable? Maybe . . . but so was Jimmy, and yet the powers-that-be had swallowed that story whole without even seeing the boy.

While reflecting on my scheme, I became conscious of how much I had changed in such a short time.

"Sister," I now realized, is an empty label unless both women want to claim kinship.

Alas, Tiffany Nixon had taught me the art of character assassination and I had always been a conscientious student.

At least I would give her a chance to salvage her career—it was far more than she had done for me.

I imagined myself lying in wait for Tiffany when she got off work late one evening and stepping out of the shadows, waving her past improprieties in her face like some evil flag.

According to the information in the folder that Pam had given me, Tiffany Nixon was born in Louisville, Kentucky, but she was an army brat. The family moved often and she didn't spend much time in any one school until she entered Mount Holyoke College in 1975. The reporter was single, asthmatic, lived on 71st Street between Broadway and West End Avenue, played the flute as a hobby, saw her parents on holidays, and didn't particularly care for her three sisters: Janus, Eleanor, and Oona. In fact, I found a two-year-old column in the folder that she wrote about her family which was downright vicious.

WE CAN'T CHOOSE OUR RELATIVES
by Tiffany Nixon

I'm from a totally screwed-up family. No, I didn't grow up in a single-parent home nor were we poor.

We just didn't like each other.

There were four girls: me, Janus, Eleanor, and Oona. I'm the youngest.

Mother's favorite was Eleanor, while Pop leaned toward Janus and Oona.

No one, including my siblings, liked me at all. Why? Because I'm the dark one. Dark as in too much melanin in the skin to suit them. And so I was ridiculed and ignored.

My parents mercifully have died, but there are still three women out there who claim sisterhood with me at their convenience. You see, as a columnist, I mingle with the rich, famous, celebrated, and infamous. My "sisters" have no problem calling or e-mailing when they want concert tickets or an introduction to someone who can help them get ahead in some way.

Sometimes I help out, but mostly I don't.

I say all of this to remind my readers to avoid fake and forced cheer during this holiday season. Spend time with people you like and who like you back. Do not feel obligated to spend time with people you detest, simply because they are biologically connected to you.

I stopped doing that a long time ago.

I will spend tomorrow opening presents with a group of my friends and enjoy myself tremendously. Please do the same.

Merry Christmas!

This was great news—if she didn't like her siblings, the feeling was probably mutual—which meant they might talk to me. The problem was, Janus lived in Philadelphia, Eleanor was overseas with her husband, Oona's home was in Kenosha, Wisconsin, and I was not allowed to leave New York State. Who would be willing to go on the road for me and what could I offer that person in return?

31

BROTHERS

I dressed like the corporate executive I used to be—a navy blue suit, flesh-colored stockings, and black pumps. No one who glanced my way would equate me with the wild-eyed creature in the televised mug shot. The restaurant/bar called Brothers was located on Hudson Street, a few blocks away.

She was nowhere in sight. I was only twenty minutes late. Had she come and gone? I described her to a passing waitress, who said she didn't remember seeing anyone who fit that description.

I passed the time sipping ginger ale at a little table away from the window and kept my back to the aging preppies enjoying Happy Hour at the bar. It was a spacious establishment with comfy armchairs, a blond wood floor, ceiling fans, and pictures of famous rock musicians like Mick Jagger, Bruce Springsteen, and Alice Cooper. A tape of their hits played quietly as a backdrop.

Alyssa Kraft showed up just as I was giving up hope. She was wearing black jeans, a gray silk tee shirt, and strappy silver sandals. A stream of apologies fell from her lips as she eased her five-foot, nine-inch frame into the seat across from me. We ordered drinks and catfish sandwiches.

"How are you, Jackie?"

I sighed. "Bewildered, scared, angry, and tired."

She looked at me with pity in her eyes. "How can I help?"

"I need you to do me a huge favor."

"Do you need money?"

"No."

We were quiet for a moment while I summoned up the nerve to ask for what I needed.

"Tell me," Alyssa said softly.

My words bumped up against each other in my hurry to get them out. "Alyssa, I don't want you to feel obligated to do this. If the idea makes you nervous, just tell me and I promise not to hold it against you."

She nodded.

The waitress set our drinks on the table. We waited until she was gone before continuing our conversation.

"What do you want me to do?"

"Some traveling."

She listened intently with her head cocked to one side.

"Philadelphia and a place in Wisconsin."

"To see . . ."

"I need you to go see two women. They are sisters, but neither one of them can know that you're in touch with the other one. You'll have to lie and say that you're an official person from the committee that awards the Pulitzer Prize. You're there to investigate the background of a reporter who is in line to receive that prize. Understand?"

"Is this reporter really in line for a Pulitzer?"

"No."

She looked wary. "This sounds illegal."

"I don't know if it is or isn't," I told her frankly.

"Go on."

"You're investigating the background of a woman named Tiffany Nixon."

"Isn't she the reporter who is always writing about you?"

"Yes. And the two women you're going to see are both her sisters. She hates them enough to write about it and I'm hoping that they feel the same way. I need anything bad they can tell you about Tiffany . . . something that would interest the editors of the *Comet.*"

She whistled. "Holy shit!"

I continued as though she hadn't spoken. "Alyssa, you'll have to work fast and you can only visit each house one time."

Alyssa swallowed a huge gulp of her drink. "When do I leave?"

We clicked glasses in a toast.

32

A NEW DEAL

Blackmail focuses the brain.

Would I ruin Tiffany Nixon's career if she didn't play ball? Was I capable of living with the guilt that would accompany such an act? I couldn't help going over and over the possible karmic results of blackmail, unsure of how big a price the universe would force me to pay.

Alyssa didn't turn up much, but combined with certain inconsistencies that had arisen from my fact-checking, it was enough for me to proceed.

How should I approach Tiffany Nixon? I weighed my choices carefully.

A letter sent through the mail was one way to do it. But I would have no way of gauging her reaction. It was also a piece of physical evidence that could be turned over to the district attorney.

Calling her was not an option. According to the file, Tiffany had a taping device attached to the phone at the office which recorded all of her incoming and outgoing calls. Did she have such a system in her home as well? I couldn't take that chance. It was clear that I'd have to pay Miss Nixon a visit.

She usually worked until six and it would be dusk before she reached her block. I wore a black sweat suit and sneakers. I put my money in my bra and my keys in my pocket. It was important to be able to run away if Tiffany sounded the alarm. Unless I was caught on her doorstep, it was a case of my word against hers. I wrote a long letter to Elaine, telling her where I was going and why, and dropped it in the mail on my way to the subway.

At seven, Tiffany Nixon turned the corner onto 71st Street. I was standing down a short flight of steps in front of a store that sold books on theater and film when she passed. I recognized her from the picture that always appeared at the top of her newspaper column.

Tiffany was about five feet-eight and weighed roughly 200 pounds. Her reddish-brown hair was thinly corn-rowed and there were silver beads at the end of each one. She was wearing a multicolored peasant dress which swirled around her ankles, showing off a pair of silver sandals.

In spite of her considerable bulk, she was an attractive woman who walked like a dancer.

I slipped from my hiding place and walked behind her until she crossed the street. Then I fell into lockstep beside her.

"Your column last year on Jesse Jackson was very interesting," I said without looking directly at her.

"Which one, honey? I do a lot of Jesse." Her voice was tired as though she'd had a hard day.

"The one on his speech at the University of Michigan. The topic was 'America Must Leave No One Behind: A Celebration of Diversity.' "

She kept walking. "Thanks, but I don't really remember it."

I jogged along beside her. "It's the one where you described sitting in the Hill Auditorium on that campus listening to Jesse drone on about the merits of affirmative action and how the place was packed so tightly that you could barely breathe."

She stopped walking. I stopped jogging.

"The one where you talked to several students after his speech was over and reported on what they had to say," I concluded.

"Who are you?" she demanded.

"Someone who knows that you were nowhere near the University of Michigan the day Jesse gave that speech. You had a big fight with your sister, Oona, the night before. The two of you continued arguing the next morning and you were late leaving her house because of it. You missed your flight to Michigan, Miss Nixon."

Tiffany Nixon didn't move. My head was down, eyes gazing at her sandaled feet.

The feet moved toward me. I backed up.

"Who the fuck are you?" she snarled. "And what do you want?"

I looked up and saw that she was coming straight at me. I stood still and let her punch me right in the mouth.

She shook me by the shoulders. "I'm going to ask you one more time . . ."

A white woman rushed up to us, dragging her poor little dog on its leash. "I saw you hit this woman, now let go of her."

Tiffany blinked and released me.

My lip was cut. I wiped my hand across it and saw blood. "Miss, could you be a witness to first-degree assault if I need you?"

The woman didn't hesitate. "Yes. My name is Josephine Harris."

My mouth felt like it was on fire. "Thank you."

"Are you going to be all right?"

"Yes. This woman won't hit me again."

She gave Tiffany a nasty look, mumbled something about New York going to hell in a handbasket, and walked on with her dog. I was just thinking that I'd forgotten to get the stranger's address when Tiffany spoke.

"Look, I shouldn't have hit you. I'm sorry."

I wanted to kick her ass. "My name is Jacqueline Blue."

Tiffany gasped and then shrieked.

"I came to see you because I need your help."

She was sputtering uselessly.

"I am not a killer. I am just an ordinary book editor who wants to go back to work. Can you understand that?"

Tiffany Nixon just glared at me.

"I've done my homework, Miss Nixon. The Jesse column was not the first time you fabricated a story." I was bluffing here—Alyssa hadn't found anything else. "That's a big deal in the newspaper business. It would cost you your job and no one else will ever hire you."

"There is no point in my going for this. You'll just come back again. Blackmailers never quit."

I hadn't expected this. "Blackmailers usually want money. I don't."

She crossed her arms and her eyes went squinty with anger. "You want me to run a column saying I don't believe you are guilty, right?"

I shook my head. "No. I want to tell you some very interesting things about this case. If you follow up on the information I give you, Annabelle's killer is going to panic and make a mistake."

I was scared to death. If my scheme backfired and Tiffany went to the police with the fact that I tried to blackmail her, whatever public support I had would disappear in a flash.

Tiffany looked interested, but she was still frowning. "I'm listening."

"Look, Miss Nixon. I was arrested on evidence that was purely circumstantial. There's a good chance that I won't be convicted of the crime but that is not good enough for me and Annabelle deserves better, too. I want my name cleared and the real murderer locked up. All I'm asking you to do is a little investigative reporting—who knows what you'll turn up?"

Her hands were now balled up into fists at her side. This was not a woman who took bullying well. "Start talking."

And so I did.

While scrubbing my makeup off that night, I glanced in the mirror. The woman who gazed back at me was someone I no longer knew.

33

THOSE WELBURN GALS

There was nothing I could do except be patient. Tiffany's column appeared every day but she didn't write anything related to the case until two weeks later. It was worth the wait.

WAS SARAH SOBBING WITH GRIEF FOR FIFTEEN MINUTES?
by Tiffany Nixon

Sarah Jane Welburn and Mike Rizzelli met seven years ago at a wedding reception. He was the caterer and she, the bride's old college chum. It didn't take long for them to become an item (those Welburn gals sure don't marry up, do they?) and their own wedding followed just a year later.

The new Mrs. Rizzelli kept her maiden name professionally and continued on with her work as an interior decorator for the Park Avenue set. Her firm, Le Magnifique, flourished over the next two years just as the forty-year-old, family-owned firm, Rizzelli Caterers, began a decline. She told her friends that Mike began to drink.

According to their neighbors on West End Avenue, the couple often had loud arguments that went on for hours.

The last fight in the apartment occurred five months ago, shortly after eight a.m., and it was so heated that someone called the police. By the time the police got there at eight-thirty, no one was home. Mr. Rizzelli was gone and Sarah Jane Welburn Rizzelli had hailed a cab for a trip to her sister's home.

According to my source, who shall remain anonymous, the argument between Sarah Jane and Mike had something to do with Annabelle. In fact, after Mike stalked out, Sarah Jane called Annabelle and "really laid into her." She was on the phone "screaming and sobbing like a crazy woman."

We've been told that Sarah Jane arrived at The Dakota at nine, too late to save her sibling, who had been strangled in her own bathroom. Annabelle's doorman called 911 at nine-fifteen.

Why didn't Sarah Jane call the police and what was she doing for fifteen whole minutes?

The column set off a firestorm of articles over the next few days. Keith, Mama, and I were elated as the press stumbled over themselves in an effort to upstage each other. *"CAIN AND ABEL?"* ran a headline in the *News*. The venerable *New York Times* featured a prim article alluding to Annabelle's rumored affairs but it was the *New York Comet* that showed Victor Bell on the front page, trying to duck the camera. The headline above him screamed *"IS THIS DORA'S DAD?"* and the story inside reported:

Annabelle Welburn Murray, the murdered debutante-turned-publisher, was involved in a torrid affair with Victor Bell, a 35-year-old African-American sales repre-

sentative for Bingham & Stone, publishers of numerous celebrity memoirs and home to several best-selling novelists.

It is believed that Mrs. Murray, doubtful that her husband was actually the biological father of their only child, subjected Dora, aged three, to DNA testing a week before she died. The results of those tests have not been released.

Although a spokesperson at Bingham & Stone refused to comment, book-publishing insiders agree that the normally taciturn Mr. Bell is "a very private individual who rarely talks about his personal life." Now they all know why.

Everyone in the Black Pack (except Joe and Victor) was trying to reach me, but I only took Elaine's calls. She was handling our project with brisk efficiency—her publisher was now in on our secret and had granted her a blank check to make the book happen.

Every single one of the news bulletins reviewed my career, arrest, and upcoming trial.

With investigative reporters from the *National Enquirer* to *Newsweek* working on the story and poking holes in both Annabelle's reputation and the district attorney's case, there was nothing left for me to do.

I had fought the good fight and now the days stretched before me. Keith was busy with jury selection, pretrial motions, and other legal maneuverings designed to save my life.

34

THE PEOPLE VS.
JACQUELINE BLUE

Paul's arm around my shoulder and Mama's presence at my side were the only things that kept me from falling apart as we marched behind Keith up the steps of the courthouse, through the hallway, into the elevator, and then out into another hallway with the media and the curious hot on our heels. I saw Tiffany Nixon and she turned her face away.

Pam and Alyssa managed to squeeze through the throng. They squeezed my hand. Alyssa whispered, "Stay strong, Jackie. Remember, we've got your back." I blinked my tears away and gave her a grateful smile.

Keith and I scrutinized the jam-packed courtroom. The only people I recognized were Tiffany Nixon and Jamal Hunt, who was peering around and scribbling on a pad. I knew that his next book would contain a remarkably realistic courtroom scene.

"Sit here," Keith said, indicating the space beside him at the defense table.

Judge Madeline Veronsky, a cherubic figure in her stern black robes, called for order in the room.

The anorexic-looking woman whom I'd last seen the

morning I was released from jail was the prosecutor. Ruth Champ paced back and forth in front of the jury throughout her opening statement.

The mouths of Veronksy and Champ were set in rigid Thin Pink Lines during the entire trial.

Champ said, "The State of New York will prove that Jacqueline Blue, with the intent to cause the death of Mrs. Annabelle Murray, did in fact cause her death; that as Mrs. Murray turned to retrieve an appointment book that the defendant claimed to have left in her home by accident, Miss Blue punched her in the back of the head, dragged Mrs. Murray into her own bathroom, and strangled her. She then ran from the building, jumped into a cab, and went to work at Welburn Books, a company that Mrs. Murray's family has owned since 1899. Why? Because Jacqueline Blue is an aggressive and hostile woman who has a gigantic chip on her shoulder, and when Annabelle Murray decided not to promote her to a higher position, that huge chip became a murder weapon."

The journalists assembled in the row in back of me scrawled rapidly, drafting pieces of writing that they would have to turn into polished articles and news reports in time for tomorrow's newspapers and early morning broadcasts.

At ten o'clock, Keith began his opening statement. "Ms. Champ has just told you that she will prove Jacqueline Blue guilty beyond a reasonable doubt. Ladies and gentlemen, I submit to you that the evidence will show that Ms. Blue did not murder anyone. She is, in fact, still mourning Mrs. Annabelle Murray, who was not only her employer, but a friend. When you have heard all of the evidence in this case, you will have to conclude that Jacqueline Blue paid her boss a visit on that fateful morning to retrieve her personal property and that when she left the apartment, Annabelle Murray was still alive and unharmed. When you have heard the testimony of those who came into contact with Ms. Blue that morning, you will conclude that Ms. Blue had no knowledge of the terrible tragedy until all the employees at Welburn Books were informed shortly before noon of that awful day. What is more, you will ultimately realize that the position Ms. Blue wanted was not worth killing for. It would have been far easier for Ms. Blue to obtain that same position at another book publishing firm."

I sat at the defense table with my hands folded in front of me like an obedient third-grader.

In a criminal trial, the prosecution presents its case first. Ruth Champ started off with a parade of forensic people, the coroner, and other scientific types to establish the gory details of Annabelle's death. On cross-examination, Keith got the coroner to admit that the person who strangled Annabelle was either a man or an extraordinarily strong woman because her larynx had been crushed.

When Astrid Norstromm took the stand, her Thin Pink Line was already in place. Champ approached her with an air of sympathy.

"Will you please state your full legal name and occupation?"

"My name is Astrid Norstromm and I'm executive editor at Welburn Books."

"How long have you worked for Welburn Books?"

"One year."

Champ gave me a withering glance and then spoke directly to Astrid. "Have you ever had the chance to interact with Miss Blue?"

Astrid glared at me before turning to face the jury. "Yes, on several occasions."

"Please face forward, Miss Norstromm."

She complied.

"Based on your interactions with Miss Blue, did you come to form an opinion of her?"

"Absolutely. She has a very bad temper and seemed to have some sort of ax to grind."

There was a hum in the courtroom.

Champ looked saddened to hear this information. "Please give us an example of the behavior that led you to form this opinion."

"About a year ago, I received an excellent book proposal from a literary agent and asked Jackie to read it and tell me what she thought of it. Two days later, I went into her office to discuss it and she came unglued. She behaved so irrationally that I was actually afraid that she was going to attack me."

"Tell the court what you mean by the word 'unglued.' "

Astrid took a deep breath. "She hit the desk with the palm of her hand, yelled at me, and told me that I should stay away from manuscripts about Black people and stick to what I know. I was verbally abused by Jackie because I am a white woman."

The hum grew louder.

"Thank you, Miss Norstromm. No further questions."

Keith moved swiftly to cross-examine. "Miss Norstromm, what was the name of this book proposal?"

"I don't remember."

He smiled pleasantly. "Do you remember what the proposal was about?"

"Sure. It concerned the dramatic rise in the number of African-Americans sent to prison in this country over the past ten years."

"Did Miss Blue say that she was upset about these jailings?"

"We didn't talk about that."

"Did she say that the author lacked the appropriate credentials to take on such a serious project?"

"No. The author was a respected journalist. There was no way that Jackie could argue that."

"But she was definitely upset."

"Yes."

"Hmmm . . . a respected journalist proposed a book about an unfortunate state of affairs affecting African-Americans. Miss Blue is an African-American who would presumably feel dismayed by the data collected by this journalist."

"That's exactly what I thought," Astrid said triumphantly.

Keith rubbed his chin. "I'm confused. Perhaps Miss Blue was offended by a position that the author took. Did the author feel that this trend is a good thing and that more Black people should be jailed?"

Ruth Champ shot out of her chair. "Objection! Miss Norstromm cannot know how this unnamed journalist feels about anything."

"Sustained."

Keith showed no sign of having heard this exchange. "Miss Norstromm, please forgive my ignorance of the publishing process. Let me ask you this: is it true that you asked Miss Blue to read the proposal because you thought that Welburn Books should enter into a contract with the author to publish the book?"

"Yes."

"What was written in this proposal that convinced you that Welburn Books should offer the author a contract?"

"It was the author's opinion that given the astonishing number of impoverished Black people in privately owned prisons, and given the fact that a large number of Black people are interested in starting their own businesses, it was only fair that wealthy, middle-class Blacks get a chance to own these prisons themselves."

The hum became a roar and the judge pounded her gavel to bring the court back to order.

"Miss Norstromm, are you an American citizen?"

"Not yet. I've applied for citizenship and am going through the process."

Keith's body was rigid but his tone was still reasonable. "What country are you from, Miss Norstromm?"

"Sweden," she replied proudly.

"A lovely country. I've been there several times."

She said nothing. The courtroom was quiet.

"How long have you lived in America?"

"Three years."

"So, you're an editor at Welburn Books who is from Sweden and has only lived in this country for three years. A woman from a country which has comparatively few Black citizens. A woman who may not quite grasp certain situations in the United States. Could it be, Miss Norstromm, that Jacqueline Blue did not become angry because you are a white woman? Could it be that Ms. Blue reacted quite strongly to your woeful ignorance of the fact that such a book would be viewed as a gigantic slap in the face by the African-American community?"

The courtroom erupted and Ruth Champ shouted "Objection!" over and over again as Keith demanded an answer.

After Judge Veronsky sustained Champ's objection, Keith said, "I have no further questions for this witness," and sat down beside me. His face was unreadable, and my taps on his hand to elicit some reassurance that we were off to a good start produced nothing.

Champ's next few witnesses were Annabelle's mother, aunt, and some cousins. She led them through their paces, and they talked about her upbringing in Scarsdale and the Vassar education. How funny, intelligent, well-read, pretty, and kind she was . . . what a loyal friend and wonderful mother she was . . . how she hoped to have another child someday, and the hole her absence had left in their lives.

By the time they were done, tears were coursing down my cheeks, some members of Annabelle's family were sobbing openly, and even my own lawyer appeared grief-stricken. He declined to cross-examine any of them.

Mama had a doctor's appointment and Paul had to go to work, so they skipped the afternoon session. Keith and I had lunch at an out-of-the-way burger joint. He ordered a grilled cheese sandwich, fries, and a cup of tea for himself. I picked at a salad that had lettuce leaves as limp as I felt.

Keith patted my hand for a moment. "I know this morning was rough, but keep your chin up. It ain't over till it's over."

"What about this afternoon?"

"Jackie, this whole thing is going to be tough, okay? Let's just hope that the outcome is favorable."

He ate silently and with gusto until I couldn't stand it anymore. "Keith, why do I have a mostly white jury?"

He poked at the slice of lemon bobbing up and down in his cup. "Because there hasn't been a case this big since O. J. Simpson. The next predominantly Black jury on a huge celebrity case involving a Black defendant will vote to convict, just to avoid criticism."

"That's crazy."

His face tensed. "The whole race thing is crazy, Jackie, but I didn't create it."

"This sounds very risky."

"We have a full-time jury consultant. He says that the next high-profile Black jury will convict just to prove to whites how impartial they can be."

"And this person thinks a predominantly white jury will vote in my favor?"

He shrugged. "We stand a better chance with them . . . particularly since she was cheating on her husband with a poor, Black man."

"Victor isn't poor."

He sighed. "Still coming to his defense, eh?"

"All I meant is that Victor probably makes about $100,000 a year . . . the same amount I was earning at Welburn."

"Baby, that's poor."

"Well, excuse me," I answered huffily.

He ignored my testiness. "This is going to be a relatively short trial. I give it two weeks at the most. Champ will walk the husband through what he knows about the morning of the murder, she'll call the taxi driver who says you were rushed and agitated when he picked you up shortly afterward. She probably doesn't want to put Sarah Jane on the stand since the press has asked what the victim's sister was doing for fifteen minutes, but she has no choice. Sarah Jane is the one who found the body. I'll call character witnesses and a private investigator for you. We'll pray that the jury believes me and wait for their verdict."

Keith didn't have to say the rest. If they didn't, I would be found guilty and spend the rest of my life in the Bedford Hills Correctional Facility for Women.

35

A FIFTEEN-MINUTE GAP

Sarah Jane Welburn Rizzelli took the stand that afternoon. She didn't look anything like her sister. Her hair was dirty blond, the face thin, its nose narrow and twitchy. She looked like a dried-up mouse sniffing around for cheese.

Louise Champ smiled warmly at her after the swearing-in. "Mrs. Rizzelli, I'm sorry to add to your troubles by bringing you here today."

"I understand." Her voice was thin, a cross between a whisper and a rice paper Japanese fan.

"I will not keep you here a moment longer than necessary."

"Thank you."

"Mrs. Rizzelli, have you ever met Jacqueline Blue?"

"No. I only know that my sister, Annabelle, was afraid of her."

There was a hissing sound from the jury box.

"Did Annabelle tell you that she was afraid of Jacqueline Blue?"

"Yes."

"When did she tell you that?"

"The night before she died."

"Please go on."

"Annabelle said that after she turned down Blue's request for a promotion, the woman made a fist at her and stalked out of her apartment without even saying good-bye. She called me and asked if she should notify the police. I said no."

I whispered to Keith, "I never made a fist at my boss and I don't believe for a second that Annabelle ever said I did. The woman is lying through her goddamned teeth. I feel like pulling her off the witness stand and pummeling her into the floor."

Keith motioned that I should be quiet.

Sarah Jane sobbed into a handkerchief.

"When was the last time you spoke with Annabelle?" asked Champ.

"The morning she died. I called while she was getting ready for work. We chatted for a few minutes, and then the doorman called from downstairs to say she had a visitor. I told her I was coming over to pick up some photos and hung up."

"And when you got there?" prodded Champ.

Sarah Jane began to cry loudly. "When I got there, my sister was dead!"

The judge, looking shaken, agreed to a brief recess and gave Keith a look that warned him not to cross-examine the witness too closely.

Keith didn't even pretend to be sympathetic when the court reconvened.

"What time did you arrive at Mrs. Murray's apartment on January 27, 1997?"

Sarah Jane looked confused. "About 9:15, I think."

Keith shook his head and picked up some papers from the defense table. "No. Jacqueline Blue left The Dakota apartment building at exactly 8:55 A.M. You came through the door at precisely 9:00."

She said nothing.

"At 9:15, you ran into the lobby and told the security guard at the front desk that your sister was injured. He called 911 and the police arrived on the scene at 9:25."

She waved her tiny hands. "It's all such a blur. I'm sure you can understand that, Mr. Williams."

"I certainly can," Keith answered cordially. "What I can't understand is the fifteen-minute lag time. Do you have a key to your sister's apartment?"

"Yes."

"Why?"

"In case of an emergency."

"What kind of an emergency?"

"In case Annabelle lost her key and couldn't get in."

Keith searched his notes as though he were confused. "But didn't her husband also share that apartment with her?"

"Yes."

"Did Craig Murray know that you had keys to his home?"

"I don't know."

"Okay. Did Annabelle unlock the door for you or did you let yourself in?"

She neatly sidestepped the trap. "My sister could not unlock the door because she was lying dead on the bathroom floor."

Keith was unperturbed. "So, you let yourself in. Then what?"

"I found her lying on her back and . . . and . . . oh, I can't go on!" She began to cry again.

Keith's voice hardened. "Did you go into the kitchen first? Her bedroom? The library? Another bathroom? Did you call her name as you walked through the apartment?"

"Objection!"

"Sustained. One question at a time, Mr. Williams."

"Would you like me to repeat the questions, one by one, Mrs. Rizzelli?"

"No."

"Then walk us through those minutes, please."

She rambled on about calling Annabelle's name as she walked through each room. The pink bathroom was the last place she checked and made the shocking discovery.

"Why didn't you call the police?"

Sarah Jane's voice cracked again. "I've asked myself that question a thousand times."

"And the answer is?" Keith persisted.

Her voice dropped to a whisper. "I don't know."

Keith bowed from the waist. "Thank you."

"Is there anything else?"

"Yes. Do you know the identity of Dora Murray's biological father?"

Sarah Jane looked wildly from Judge Veronsky to Ruth Champ and back again. "What is the meaning of this?"

"Yes, Counselor," Judge Veronsky spoke sharply from the bench. "What is the point of your question?"

"I have reason to believe," Keith said smoothly "that Annabelle Murray knew that her husband did not father their little girl, Dora. It is also my understanding that the witness quarreled with her sister about this very issue during a phone call on the morning of the murder."

"May I approach the bench?" Ruth Champ yelled.

There was a fifteen-minute delay while Keith and Ruth argued in front of the judge. When it was over, Keith had lost.

"The jury will disregard that last question," instructed Veronsky.

Keith nodded. "Did you quarrel with your sister by phone on the morning of her death?"

"Yes."

"What was the argument about?"

"Annabelle had some old family photos that were rightfully mine."

"Did she know that you were stopping by that morning?"

"Yes."

"To get the pictures?"

"What do you mean?"

Keith sighed. "Let me rephrase the question. Why did you go to your sister's house on the morning of the murder?"

Sarah Jane shifted uncomfortably in the witness chair. "Because Annabelle asked me to."

"What did she want that could not wait until a less busy time? After all, you were both heading off to work."

"Annabelle wanted me to take the pictures right away so we wouldn't have that argument again."

"Isn't it true that there was someone in the apartment with Annabelle when you spoke to her on the phone that morning?"

Sarah Jane hesitated. "Craig wasn't home. He left the night before and didn't come back."

"I'm not talking about your sister's husband," Keith said softly. "Who was the man who made Annabelle cry only minutes before she died?"

Champ objected and the judge agreed. Keith let Sarah Jane go. Craig was next. His hair, dress, manner, and posture were confident and fit neatly with his new job as Chief Executive Officer of a major New York publishing house. His testimony was brief, sad, and inconsequential.

Paul had to stay late at the office and didn't get home till nearly eight. I was already in bed, just lying there trying to figure out whether Keith and I were winning or losing.

He crossed the threshold without saying a word and dumped a manuscript on the floor.

He sat down beside me and rubbed his temples.

"What's the matter?" I asked.

"I'm exhausted," he answered.

"Have you had dinner?"

"A slice of pizza on the way in."

"Are you still hungry?"

He stood up and started to undress. "No. I just need some sleep."

"Paul?"

"Yes?"

"Are the powers-that-be giving you a hard time at work?"

He unzipped his pants. "Nothing I can't handle."

Although Paul's tone was flippant, I knew that things had to be pretty serious—he hadn't even kissed me. The tabloids had been running his photo, hinting that he was my lover, right along with mine ever since my release from jail. No company wanted one of its key employees to be linked to an accused murderess. This awful mess was going to cost Paul his job.

"I'm sorry," I told him softly.

He was standing in his drawers now. "Don't worry about it, baby. How was court this afternoon?"

I told him about Sarah Jane's testimony and the change in Craig.

"What does Keith make of all this?"

"I have no idea."

Paul crawled up on the bed beside me and kissed me three times—on the forehead, nose, and lips. "The brother definitely doesn't show his hand."

I sighed. "Not at all."

His hand snaked under the nightgown and started

rubbing my thigh. "We're both all stressed out. Maybe there's a way to work off some of this tension."

My nose wrinkled. "Man, you didn't even take a shower yet."

He groaned and hoisted himself back to a standing position. "After that water hits me, I won't be good for anything."

"That's okay," I smiled. "We have hundreds of nights ahead of us, right?"

He paused in the doorway and our eyes locked. "You're worried that I'm having second thoughts about all this, aren't you?"

I nodded, unable to speak.

"Well, I'm not. Nothing is ever going to come between us."

I blinked back tears of relief. "You're the greatest."

"I love you, too, Jackie." He winked and left the room.

36

THE SHOWMAN, PART I

Paul and Mama insisted on coming to court the next morning even though I told them that it wasn't necessary.

Ruth Champ was grinning like a Cheshire cat, and the sight made my stomach drop. What did she have up her sleeve?

And then Joe Long took the stand. He was wearing a gray suit, white shirt, and gray tie.

Champ had him state his full name and occupation.

"Mr. Long, how well do you know Jacqueline Blue?"

Joe shrugged. "We're not what I'd call friends. She is a fellow editor and we saw each other at business-related gatherings."

"What is your opinion of Miss Blue?"

"I think she is mentally unstable."

Keith let this testimony go unchallenged, and when I tugged frantically at his sleeve, he pushed my hand away.

"What makes you say that, Mr. Long?"

"Because she pursued my best friend relentlessly for a year. There are laws against stalking someone who doesn't want to be bothered and I told him to get the police involved, but he refused."

"What is your friend's name?"

"Victor Bell."

There was a rustle among the reporters. The media had been chewing over the Dora's Dad angle like a dog with a meaty bone.

"Do you like Miss Blue?"

"No."

"Why not?"

"She was never friendly to me, even though we saw each other every week at our networking group."

Champ gave the jury a summary. "So, in your opinion, Jacqueline Blue is a cold woman who does not know how to take no for an answer."

"Exactly."

Champ smirked in Keith's direction. "Your witness."

Keith stepped up to the plate and went straight for the jugular. "You love him, don't you, Mr. Long?"

Joe started coughing and the proceedings came to a halt as Keith waited for him to drink some water.

"I don't understand the question, sir."

"Do you love Mr. Victor Bell?"

"He is my best friend. I care about him."

Keith laughed and the sound was nasty. "Okay, have it your way."

I remembered my confusion when Dallas said that Joe was jealous of me. Now it made sense. Joe was in love with Victor and was only playing the buddy role to stay close to a man he could not have.

"Did you ever meet Annabelle Murray?"

"No."

"Did you ever talk to her on the phone?"

Joe hesitated.

"You are under oath, Mr. Long."

"Once."

"Tell us about it, please."

"I was at Victor's apartment once and she called to speak with him. I answered the phone."

"Do you know what she and Victor talked about?"

"No. He took the phone in the bathroom."

"When did this happen?"

"The night before she died."

"Did you and Victor have a conversation about Annabelle after he came out of the bathroom?"

"No. I went straight home."

Keith looked at the jury and then back at Joe. "What if I told you that there is a witness who says you and Victor had a terrible argument that night?"

"I'd say this person is lying."

Keith continued as though Joe had not spoken. "This witness overheard Mr. Bell arguing in his apartment with someone he called Joe on the night before Annabelle Murray died."

"So what? I'm not the only Joe on earth. Maybe Victor had someone else over after I left."

Keith rubbed his forehead. "Hmmmm. I guess it's possible. What time did you leave Mr. Bell's apartment?"

"About ten."

"Did you walk out of the building alone?"

"Yes."

"The neighborhood watch has a surveillance camera on that corner," Keith said gently. "I'll ask you one more time. Did you walk out of that building alone?"

Joe dropped his head. "No."

"Who was with you?"

"Victor."

Keith paused. "Did Victor take you home?"

"No."

"Did you ask Victor to walk out with you?"

"I don't remember."

"Sure you do," Keith yelled. "Isn't it true that Victor Bell said that he was going to Annabelle's house?"

"I don't remember."

Champ shouted, "Objection! The question has been asked and answered."

The judge sustained her objection.

Keith's voice became sympathetic. "You're a good friend, Joe. Too bad Victor doesn't appreciate you. I think you've been trying to keep Victor away from Annabelle for a long time. Am I right?"

Joe sighed. "Yes."

"Why?"

"Because he was in love and she wasn't. Because she used him as a plaything for her own amusement, and I didn't see how any good could come of the whole affair."

"So, you argued with Victor when he said he was going to Annabelle's apartment on the night before she died because you were afraid for him. Correct?"

"Yes."

Keith sighed. "One last question. If you knew that Victor and Annabelle were having a sexual relationship, why did you become so angry on this particular night?"

Joe looked up at the ceiling as he answered in a dry monotone. "Victor told me a few weeks before the murder that Annabelle had grown bored with the whole thing and wouldn't see him anymore. I believed him until one of our friends saw him coming out of Victoria's Secret on Madison Avenue with a bunch of packages. I asked him about it and he stuck to his story but I knew he was lying. That night when she called and he told me they were meeting at her apartment, I was shocked. I mean, screwing a man's wife in a hotel is one thing but it is stupid to meet in a married man's home and I told him so. Victor told me to mind my own business and things got heated."

"Did you and Victor talk about what happened that night at Annabelle's apartment?"

"No. Even after she got killed, we never talked about her again."

"Thanks. I have no further questions."

My mind was reeling. What did all this mean, and why was Keith preening and smirking at me like the case was over?

The next morning, I gasped when Ruth Champ stood up and said, "The state calls Victor Bell." The story of my obsession was about to unfold.

My hands started to shake and I had to lean on Keith's shoulder to keep from fainting. After Victor was sworn in, Champ began her questioning.

"Mr. Bell, what do you do for a living?"

"I'm a sales representative for Bingham & Stone Publishers."

"Will you please tell the court what your duties are?"

"Basically, I'm one of a team of people who travel to bookstores across the country and try to get the stores to order as many of Bingham's titles as possible."

"Do you know Jacqueline Blue?"

"Of course."

"Are you friends?"

He didn't hesitate. "Yes, I consider Jackie a friend."

Champ shouted, "You're a very kind man, Mr. Bell. It takes a man with a very good heart to tolerate what you've had to put up with over the past year and still call the woman a friend."

Keith leapt to his feet so fast, my head almost dropped to the bench. "Objection, your honor!"

The judge frowned. "Objection sustained. The jury will disregard Ms. Champ's last remarks."

Champ apologized.

"Do you have a line of questioning for this witness or not, Ms. Champ?"

"Yes, Your Honor."

"Then ask your questions."

Champ turned back to Victor.

"Were you ever romantically involved with Miss Blue?"

"No."

Tell me this, were you ever interested in dating Miss Blue?"

"No."

"Did she ever express an interest in dating you?"

"Yes."

"Would it be fair to say that Miss Blue has pursued you relentlessly via e-mail in an effort to become your girlfriend?"

"Yes."

"At some point, did you ask her to stop contacting you?"

"No."

"Why not?"

"We work in the same industry. I didn't want to hurt her feelings."

"Did Miss Blue send you a suggestive e-mail shortly before the murder?"

"Yes."

"Tell us about it."

"It wasn't like the others, where she just talked on and on about her life. This one was bold. She indicated that she wanted me to make love to her."

Oh, the humiliation! I put my head down on my arms and wept right there at the defense table until Keith's insistent whispering that I pull myself together made me sit up straight.

"Did you accept her invitation, Mr. Bell?"

"No."

"Why not?"

"I figured that if I had sex with her, she would bug me even more, but her invitation really irked me so my reply to her e-mail was kind of mean. I'm sorry about it now. Jackie is really a nice person."

Champ walked purposefully over to the prosecution table and picked up three pieces of paper which the judge allowed her to admit into evidence. She then addressed the jury. "Allow me to read Exhibit #1, an e-mail from Jacqueline Blue to Victor Bell:

Hi, Handsome,
  Sorry you missed the Black Pack meeting last night. I was looking forward to seeing you. Suppose we both skip next Friday's gathering and get together alone at my place. I'll wear something sheer and pour Dom Perignon into real crystal glasses while we . . . er . . . talk."

There was a flurry of activity in the courtroom and a few giggles. I stared at my hands.

She continued. "And now, Exhibit #2, Victor Bell's reply:

Dear Jackie:
  I have my hands full with my new girlfriend and career. Thank you for the offer but I'm not looking for THAT.
  If you have any business-related requests, I will help you if I can."

There was a gasp from somewhere in the back of the room. Was it my mother?

Champ held another paper high above her head for a moment so that everyone could see it. "This is Jacqueline Blue's answer to Mr. Bell's refusal:

Victor:
  I have never been kicked in the stomach by a steel-toed boot, but it can't possibly hurt more than your last message.

She handed all three papers over to the clerk and turned back to Victor.

"Mr. Bell, do you have a steady girlfriend?"

"No."

"Would it be fair for me to say that you lied to Miss Blue about having one to avoid having sex with her?"

"Yes."

"Did you ever tell her that stalking someone who is clearly not interested in that attention is against the law?"

Keith objected and the judge sustained, so Victor couldn't answer that question.

"How did you feel when Miss Blue compared your refusal to being kicked by a steel-toed boot?"

Victor shrugged. "I figured she'd be mad at me for a couple of months and then e-mail me again."

"In other words, she was obsessive and relentless. Correct?"

Victor sighed. "Yes."

"Thank you—no further questions."

I begged Keith not to cross-examine Victor but he just shrugged me off and sauntered up to the witness stand.

"Good morning, Mr. Bell."

"Good morning, Mr. Williams."

"Can we drop the formality just a little? I'd like you to call me Keith and I'll call you Victor. Would that be all right with you?"

"Yes."

"Okay, Victor. Did I hear you say a moment ago that you do not have a steady girlfriend?"

"Yes."

"In other words, after Annabelle Murray was murdered, you were too grief-stricken to take on another lover?"

"Yes."

"So you freely admit that at the time of her death, you and Annabelle Murray were lovers?"

"Yes."

"Were you aware that Annabelle Murray was a married woman?"

"Yes."

"And it didn't bother you?"

Victor shrugged. "I didn't know her husband."

"How long did this adulterous affair last?"

"Six years."

"During that time, did you ever tell Jacqueline Blue that you were sleeping with her boss?"

"No."

"Why not?"

"It wasn't any of her business."

"Fair enough. Let's talk about the Black Pack. Will you please tell the court what that group is about?"

"It isn't really an official group or anything. It's just a bunch of us in publishing who get together for dinner and drinks on Friday nights when we don't have to work late. I missed a lot of the gatherings because I'm on the road a lot."

"A bunch of Black people, correct?"

"Yes."

"How many?"

"About seven or eight, I guess."

"The number is eight, Victor. Eight Black people. Why don't you tell us why the Black Pack came into existence?"

Victor hemmed and hawed. "I don't . . . uh . . . uh . . . I can't remember."

Keith stroked his chin. "Are there any secretaries or mailroom workers in the Black Pack?"

"No."

"Assistant editors, trainees, interns, receptionists, or support staff of any kind?"

"No."

"So, would it be fair to say that the eight of you comprise the total number of Black managers working in New York's book publishing industry?"

"Yes."

"Was Ms. Blue a member of that group?"

"Yes."

"Did the eight of you create programs designed to get more Blacks into New York book publishing?"

"No. It was just like . . . a social group."

Keith pounced. "A social group? Then you didn't talk about book publishing or the people in it at all. Is that your testimony, Victor?"

"No, we talked about everything."

"Were white publishing professionals ever invited to these social gatherings?"

"I don't know."

"Stop lying, Victor."

Champ said, "Objection! That is not a question."

"Sustained," droned Judge Veronsky.

"Isn't it true that the weekly Black Pack meetings were a place for its eight African-American members to air their grievances against the white publishing establishment?"

I cringed at this last question and felt sorry for my colleagues who were going to pay a stiff price for it.

Victor hung his head. "Yes."

"Isn't it true that you talked about the Black Pack meetings with Mrs. Murray?"

"Yes."

"I'll bet you two had a good laugh at the expense of your seven friends, didn't you, Victor?"

"Objection!"

"Sustained."

Keith's voice dripped with sarcasm. "Isn't it true that you snuck around with a white married woman and had sex with her during the week, not caring about the harm you were doing to her white husband and little child, and then met with the Black Pack on Friday nights to speak out against white people?"

There was a roar in the courtroom and Judge Veronsky banged the gavel until it seemed her hand was about to fall off.

Champ was screaming her objections, the courtroom was buzzing like ten hives of bees. The judge agreed with Champ and Victor didn't have to answer the last question, but it didn't matter. Keith had made his point that Victor couldn't be trusted.

"Did you come into contact with Miss Blue at these Black Pack meetings during the time period when you were getting lots of e-mails from her at home?"

"Yes."

"Did she mention these e-mails that you refused to answer when she ran into you at these weekly meetings?"

"No. She acted the same as all the other women who attended. Strictly professional."

Keith clapped his hands. "Good! I'm glad to hear that my client is capable of controlling her emotions, even when she seems to want something very badly!"

Keith made a great show of walking up and down in front of the witness stand, throwing his arms out as though he were confused and seeking answers from the audience.

"Victor, did there come a time when you did, in fact, accept an invitation to Miss Blue's home?"

"Yes."

Victor was loosening his tie and wiping sweat from his forehead with his hands. Keith gave him a handkerchief without comment.

"Please tell the court how and why you came to be in Ms. Blue's apartment."

"Objection!" shouted Champ.

Judge Veronsky looked sternly at Keith over her glasses. "Is there a point to this line of questioning?"

"Yes, Your Honor. If the court will just bear with me a moment longer, my point will become crystal clear."

"Overruled—the witness may answer the question."

And so Victor told the story of the Black Pack party and how I approached him to spend the night with me. I could feel the pain in Mama's eyes drilling into the back of my head.

"Did you go to Ms. Blue's apartment that night intending to have sexual intercourse with her?"

"Yes."

"Why?"

"To be nice."

Keith threw his hands in the air. "What? It has been your testimony here today that Jacqueline Blue had been making unwanted advances for close to a year. Is that correct?"

"Yes."

"So you decided to be nice and have sex with her? Did you expect her to leave you alone after that night?"

Victor hesitated. "No . . . I . . . uh . . . it was a spur-of-the-moment decision. I didn't really think it through."

"Was there another reason besides being nice enough to have sex that you accepted Miss Blue's invitation that night?"

"No."

"Did you question her about the homicide investigation?"

"I don't remember."

"Let me rephrase the question," Keith said calmly. "Isn't it true that the real reason you went to Ms. Blue's apartment after the Black Pack party was because you wanted to find out how close the police were to finding Mrs. Murray's killer?"

"Objection!" yelled Champ.

The judge hesitated and then ruled in Keith's favor. "Answer the question, Mr. Bell."

Victor's body seemed to fold in on itself like a big helium balloon that has been punctured with a letter opener. "Yes."

I prayed fervently that Keith would drop this line of questioning. There was no need for Mama to hear that Victor had vomited after climbing into bed with me.

"Did you have sexual intercourse with Jacqueline Blue that night?"

"No."

"Why not?"

Victor sighed. "We went into her bedroom and got undressed. We climbed into her bed. There was a picture on her nightstand. I knocked it over accidentally. When I picked it up, I saw that it was Annabelle. I got upset and had to leave Jackie's house."

Keith was a real showman. He yelled, sneered, laughed sarcastically, occasionally slipped into the cadence of a Baptist preacher, waved his arms about, and paced the courtroom like he owned it.

"Did you get the information that you wanted from Jackie?"

"No. She played it real cagey and wouldn't open up about the investigation. It sort of pissed me off."

"Were you in love with Annabelle Murray?"

"Yes."

"Did she ever tell you that she loved you?"

"Once, a long time ago."

At that point, Judge Veronsky became ill and court was adjourned for the day. Unfortunately, it was a Friday afternoon, which meant that Victor's testimony was not over. He'd have to get back on the witness stand first thing Monday morning.

37

A BROKEN HEART

I couldn't stand Paul during the next few days. He seemed angry, hostile, and brittle. I knew that Victor's revelations were bothering him but he didn't want to talk.

Mama wasn't much better—several times I caught her staring at me as though I was a stranger. We were in her kitchen trying to talk about anything except the trial. Finally, I couldn't take it any longer.

"What is your problem?" I snapped.

She was washing collard greens in the kitchen sink. It seemed like she had been waiting for my question. "What was you doin' sendin' computer mail to some man who didn't want to take you out? Huh? Where did you learn how to act like that? You sure as hell didn't get it from me."

"I was just lonely, Mama. That is still no reason to tip-toe around here acting like I'm a serial killer."

She wiped her hands on her apron and turned the water off. "Serial killers are sick people. You supposed to have good sense."

"And you're supposed to stand by me, no matter what," I cried.

Mama went ballistic. Stomped her foot and beat the kitchen counter with her fist. "What I been doin' these last six months? I ain't been standin' by you?"

She didn't wait for an answer.

"I been walkin' the floor at nights, duckin' questions from everybody on this block, includin' Elvira, and watchin' all your dirty laundry get spread out all on the TV. Married men and all! It's almost August and I still don't know whether you goin' to jail or not. And you know what else?"

I didn't want to hear any more so I said nothing.

"There's a whole lot more goin' on that you ain't tole me. I can smell it an' it don't smell good at all."

The stench in her nose was blackmail, the secret book that Elaine was managing, which Keith didn't even know about, and the way I had coaxed Pam Silberstein and Alyssa Kraft into my web of deceit.

"Mama, I don't know what to say."

"Don't say nothin' 'cuz it'll prob'ly be a lie."

That stung.

"What was I supposed to do, Mama? If I played fair, you'd be making trips to an upstate prison for the next twenty-five years."

She gazed at me like I was trash. "That's where you're wrong. I ain't visitin' nobody in no prison at no time."

Mama was just upset. I didn't believe her for a minute.

"What would you have done in my place, Mama?"

"I woulda told Annabelle to stick that Moms Mabley book where the sun don't shine, that's what. You're in this mess 'cuz you was goin' along with a plan that you knew was wrong an' you did it just to get a promotion."

"That's not true," I protested wearily.

"Yes, it is. You told me yourself that if you knew the

promotion had already gone to that white girl, you woulda stuck to your guns that day at Annabelle's house. That means if Annabelle woulda gave you the new job, her an' her husband could have sent Moms Mabley's soul to hell an' you wouldn't have said nary a word. When you read that first writin' that man did on that book, you coulda walked away an' worked at the supermarket if you had to. Then you wouldn't been in that house to pick up no appointment book when Annabelle got killed. Greed is why you in this mess. Plain old greed."

She went back to cleaning the collards, but this time her tears were mixed in with the running water. "Me an' you never had much in the way of money," she sobbed, "but we did have our good name an' the neighbors respected us. Now all that's gone."

I took a long walk around Hell's Kitchen, but the familiar streets and buildings only mocked me. *Did you really think you could get away from us?* they seemed to ask.

38

THE SHOWMAN, PART II

Victor looked like he hadn't slept all weekend. He paused as he mounted the steps to the witness box and looked back over his shoulder at me. His lips moved and it looked like he was mouthing the words, *I'm sorry.*

Keith whispered in my ear. "The brother's ready to crack. This is going to be a cakewalk."

After Victor was resworn in, Keith took his place.

"How are you feeling today, Victor?"

"Fine."

"Did you have a good weekend?"

It was a cat playing with a mouse and awful to watch. Why couldn't Keith just hit Victor with a trump card and get it over with?

"Yes."

"Did you visit your daughter?"

"Daughter?"

"Sure," Keith said smoothly. "Little Dora Murray is your daughter, isn't she?"

"So I've been told."

Keith stopped in midstride. "Really? Who told you that?"

"Annabelle."

A man in the courtroom cried out, "Dear God," and I knew it was Craig. My heart ached for him.

"When did Annabelle tell you that?"

"Two weeks before she died. I told her that I wanted DNA tests for me and Dora plus visitation rights if it all checked out."

"We've had testimony from Joe Long that you went to see Annabelle in her apartment the night before she died. Is that true?"

"Yes."

"Tell us about that visit."

Victor squirmed in his chair. "Well, she called that night and said that she and Craig were getting a divorce. She was crying and upset. They had had a fight and Craig stormed out, taking Dora and some clothes with him. She said she had something important to tell me and that I had to come over right away. Annabelle had never invited me over to her house before, so I knew things were really bad. I figured Craig had found out about us or something."

"Did Annabelle tell you what the fight was about?"

"Not on the phone. She waited until I got there."

"Okay. Go on."

"Well, I told Joe where I was going, and then I took off. When I got there she was in a different mood. She said she was looking forward to being a single woman again and that she would give Craig some time to find a new place."

Keith interrupted the flow. "So at this point, you are inside Annabelle's apartment, correct?"

"Yes."

"Go on."

"I asked her what the fight was about and she told me that Dora wasn't Craig's kid. She had just found out for sure a few days before and felt he had the right to know. When she told him, he stormed out, taking the kid with him."

"What did you say to this?"

"I didn't know what to say. At first I didn't understand what she was trying to tell me. She started laughing and said, 'You dolt. I'm trying to tell you that you're a daddy.' I didn't like being called a dolt, but that was just Annabelle's way."

"What happened next?"

"I was real happy about the news, you know? I'm thirty-six years old and it's nice to know that I have a daughter. Annabelle pulled out a whole bunch of photo albums and showed me all Dora's pictures. After that we had some drinks, and then I went back home."

"What time did you go home?"

"About four in the morning."

Keith banged the ledge in front of Victor. "Do you realize that you are under oath?"

"Yes."

"Then why did you just lie to this court?"

Champ objected. The judge overruled her.

"I didn't lie."

"Sure, you did," Keith replied pleasantly. "Isn't it true that you did not leave Annabelle's apartment until after the police removed her body from the bathroom?"

Judge Veronsky had to bang the gavel three times and threaten to clear the room before order was restored.

"Objection!" yelled Champ.

"Overruled," droned Judge Veronsky. "The witness will answer the question."

"No, that is not true." Victor was sobbing loudly now.

"You skipped an important part of your conversation with Annabelle."

"What do you mean?"

"Isn't it true that Annabelle Murray offered you one million dollars that night to sign away any claim to Dora and get out of town?"

"That's a lie."

Keith's voice dripped with disgust. "Oh, really? Your Honor, I'd like to recall Joe Long to the stand."

Victor threw up his hands. "There's no need to do that. Yes, Annabelle offered me the money, but I refused her offer."

Keith smiled broadly. "Good. Now we're getting somewhere."

"I didn't kill her!" Victor shouted.

"We'll come back to that," Keith replied. "For now, I just want you to think about the time you left Annabelle's apartment. We know that the fight over the money and relinquishing your parental rights took up a couple of hours. Would you say that you left at the same time Sarah Jane Rizzelli was on her way upstairs?"

"Maybe."

"How did you get out of the building, Victor?"

"What do you mean?"

"I mean that I have the video surveillance tape, which shows everyone that came into and went out of that front door starting at five that morning. You are not on that tape. How did you get out of the building?"

"I don't remember," Victor said sullenly.

"Does the name George Jakes ring a bell?"

Victor looked genuinely confused. "No, it doesn't."

"Perhaps he didn't tell you his name. He is the maintenance man who let you out through the service entrance. By that time, Annabelle Welburn Murray was lying dead in the bathroom. You slipped George five twenty-dollar bills for the favor. Surely you remember him now, right, Victor?"

Victor said nothing.

"The witness will answer," Veronsky said.

"Yes." It was a whisper.

"Would you speak up, please?"

Loudly. "I said yes."

Keith stared at the jury, at the reporters, at me, and at the judge before whirling around and jabbing his finger in the direction of Victor's chest. "Why did you kill Annabelle Murray?"

"I respectfully wish to exercise my Fifth Amendment privilege against self-incrimination."

Keith asked several more questions and got the same answer from Victor each time.

The state and the defense rested and my case went to a jury. It took them only half an hour to come back with a verdict of "not guilty."

The reporters went running for the door with pads and pencils in hand. I gripped the edge of the defense table, practically unable to breathe.

I didn't jump up and down, cry, or show any reaction at all (the media later analyzed this fact ad nauseam) because there were just too many people like Mama and Craig who were in pain—their image of the people they loved had been shattered and it was going to take a long, long time for their hurt to subside.

39

THE ROAD AHEAD

Murder is a crime against God and humanity, and the only reason Victor committed such a heinous act was because Annabelle Murray was through with him. He loved her but the affair was over. It was a case of, if I can't have you, nobody can. He went to trial and was sentenced to life in prison without the possibility of parole. His mother is fighting for custody of Dora, who is living with her Aunt Sarah Jane, and Keith is watching that legal wrangling with great interest. He says the fight among Craig, Victor's family, and the Welburns will raise all sorts of interesting scholarly issues, and the verdict will create a gigantic legal precedent.

Craig Murray offered me my old job back at Welburn Books, but it felt too weird and I graciously declined. He kept insisting that he wanted to do something for me, so I asked him to cancel the publication of *All About Moms*. He reluctantly agreed.

After the trial, I needed somewhere to live, and staying on at Keith's place was not an option. Apparently, the brownstone only worked as a tax shelter if it were used for business purposes, and I was no longer his client.

Paul asked me to move in with him and I did. He makes me feel safe, secure, and protected. I also respect and admire my fiancé. Even though that is not the same as head-over-heels romantic love, it is a better foundation for marriage.

It felt good to witness Mama's transition from poverty to wealth. I gave her all the advance money that I received for the book and watched the worry lines disappear from her forehead and around her mouth like a magician had erased them.

How will Paul and I spend our days? Keith offered us a two-million-dollar loan to start our own publishing house and we gratefully accepted. Elaine Garner heard about my business plans and called to remind me that I owed her a story before taking on anything else. Well, this book is done now. I hope it lands on the best-seller lists and gets Elaine the big-time job that she trained for at Harvard.